Hallowed Ground

Also by Darrel Sparkman

Hallowed Ground

A Coble Bray Western Mystery
Book 1

Darrel Sparkman

WOLFPACK
PUBLISHING
— EST 2013 —

Hallowed Ground
Paperback Edition
Copyright © 2024 (As Revised) Darrel Sparkman

Wolfpack Publishing
701 S. Howard Ave. 106-324
Tampa, Florida 33609

wolfpackpublishing.com

Paperback ISBN 978-1-63977-338-1
eBook ISBN 978-1-63977-337-4

Hallowed Ground

Chapter One

COBLE BRAY RESTED ON A LIMESTONE SHELF, weathered flat by the erosion of time and high water, looking over a slow-moving creek. Tendrils of fog drifted over the water in the early morning coolness. The sun would soon chase the fog away. What little breeze there was came from the west, and he could faintly hear the lowing of cattle, guessing someone was moving a herd north.

The willow tree behind him offered shade from the sun and filtered the smoke from the small fire he used to boil water. It was a chore to dig out the tin kettle from his pack, especially in the middle of the day, and he was careful to only build a fire big enough to warm it. Large fires bring unwanted attention. But he needed the water for coffee, and to clean the wound picked up at a no-name settlement corral earlier in the week while trying to serve a warrant to a couple of men wanted for murder.

The men didn't like the idea much, and they'd brought friends to help lodge their objections.

Waiting for the water to boil, he idly watched a line-side bass chase a dragonfly, who'd wandered too close to the water's surface, break clear of the placid creek only to fall back into the water without a meal. For this creek to have a pool so wide, a beaver or two must have built a dam downstream—a fruit-less project since these small creeks were subject to flooding during heavy rains that would wash away their efforts. He chuckled. At least they'd have job security the rest of their lives—before some coyote or big cat caught them away from the safety of the water.

Frowning, he raised the side of his shirt. It wasn't much of a wound, just a crease along his ribs, but it hurt like hell. What he didn't need was cloth sticking to the wound or the shallow slice getting infected. There was a sawbones in Kansas City, but that might be a few days away, and he was used to doing things on his own.

The sound of the bass breaking water again, and his grumbling stomach, made up his mind. He rose and walked to his horse that was reined to a weeping willow. Old Red liked the shade too. He nipped at Coble as he went toward his saddlebags, probably thinking they were leaving. He swatted the horse on the nose.

"I'm just getting my bags, Red. Go back to sleep." He carried the heavy bags and as an afterthought, his bedroll and oversized canteen, back to the fire. This would be a good place to rest for a while.

Taking out a clean white rag, he tossed it into the open pot of boiling water and then got out a bottle labeled Sloan's Horse Liniment. He wasn't going to like this—really, really wasn't going to like this.

He pulled his heavy-bladed knife and stuck the blade in the boiling water. After a few minutes, he used it to lift the cloth and let it cool for a moment. Gritting his teeth, he lifted his shirt and cleaned the crease on his side. The bullet had cut through the meat just under his short ribs and left a burning gash. Satisfied the wound was clean and thankful it hadn't penetrated his belly, he pulled the cork from the liniment bottle. He looked doubtfully at the horse on the label.

Hell, if it works on a horse...

Pouring some on a clean corner of the rag, he took a deep breath and applied it to the cut.

Old Red flinched at the sound of the barely suppressed screech that came from his owner. For a moment, everything was quiet except for Coble's deep breathing. Even the birds stopped their chatter and he distinctly heard another fish hit the water. A few minutes later, things returned to normal, except for Red grinning at him. He put all the gear back into the leather saddlebags.

The sun climbed in the sky and the temperature with it, and his stomach growled again. He cut a long and limber branch from the willow and got out his fishing rig, which consisted of long twine and a fishhook. The water just below the rock was shady and cool, and the bass would come there to hide from the heat. It took a few minutes with a piece of red flannel cloth for a lure, but he snagged a couple of medium-sized fish for the pan. The heads, tails, and guts went back into the creek for the turtles to eat. With a couple of hardtack biscuits thrown into the grease and a sigh, he was content.

Sidestepping a foot stomp from Red, he retrieved his rifle and sat with his back against a rock to clean his guns. The .44-caliber Henry was old by 1878 standards, but like his Navy pistols that had been re-chambered for metal cartridges, he was used to them. They felt right, and that was important in the many gun scrapes he'd dealt with as a deputy US marshal.

He was used to being sent on special assignments, but that meant more trouble, not less. And even if he hadn't been a marshal, he seemed to have a knack for stepping from the frying pan into the fire.

Kansas City was north and east of him, and once he got there, he'd have a few days' rest. He knew a few ladies in the saloons who could offer comfort, but since the loss of his wife, he just didn't have much interest in that. He'd lost the one thing he longed for most—a good woman and family life. He'd had it once and wanted it again. But deep down inside, he felt it wouldn't happen. He didn't believe, like some folks, that there was a magic bullet out there with his name on it. The happenstance of his death would only occur when he got outsmarted or turned old and slow. Or maybe just a run of bad luck. Eventually his number would turn up, and God would say, *"Everyone has to die, and it's your turn."*

He gathered up his gear, abruptly deciding not to spend the night in this place. It was too comfortable, and for some reason, he was on edge. His inner reflections had made him morose and he felt the urge to move.

Besides...he needed a beer.

He was tightening the cinch on Red's saddle when he heard them coming, slow and easy. Easing his pistols in their holsters, with his right hand near his belly gun, Coble calmly waited. The noise stopped a few yards out.

"Hello the camp." The voice came through in a soft drawl in a matter-of-fact tone.

His reply was immediate. "Come ahead if you're friendly."

Two men rode slowly into view. Both had their hands near their pistols, but in this situation, he'd do the same. He could tell they were working cowhands just by their dress and manner. Both wore wide-brimmed hats bordering on sombrero size, covering weathered faces with piercing eyes and faded shirts tucked into homespun pants. Their leather chaps were weathered and scratched. Leather, hand-braided, California-style riatas were looped next to the oversized pommels of their saddles—and again, they'd seen a lot of use.

Coble relaxed and walked out in front of his horse, keeping a tight hold on the reins. Not that the horse would run away. Red was a back-biter but loyal. "I just broke camp, or I'd offer you boys some coffee."

The larger man nodded. "Just our luck." He gestured at the other man. "This here's Otis. I'm Jake Wheeler. We got a mixed herd yonder we're pushing up to KC and the stockyards. We figured to see if any strays were along this creek."

One glance at their horses showed a JW brand, and it made him relax a little more. "I didn't see any, but then I haven't been up or down the creek, just came straight to it."

He knew the routine. Any cow outfit was always looking for unbranded strays that lacked ownership and would round them up as they went. "You boys are a little east of the normal track, but you'll catch the Kansas Pacific a little farther north. There'll be some holding grounds to the east if they're not already grazed out. You're on the home stretch."

Jake offered him a friendly plug of tobacco before he spoke, which Coble politely refused. It was a habit he'd not acquired.

"Much obliged for the information," Wheeler said. "Actually, we came over here because we thought we heard a catamount screech a while ago. You know how it is...sounds like a woman screaming." The man paused a moment. "You seen any big cats? Wouldn't want them to scratch up the cattle."

Coble smiled sourly at them and then pointed at the red smudge on his shirt. He figured they'd already seen it and were pushing a little cow pusher humor at him. Both men looked like they were trying to hold in a smile.

"After I cleaned up this scratch, I put some Sloan's on it." He scowled at them. "That explain things to your satisfaction?"

Both men grimaced. Anyone who rode a horse knew about liniment, and it was a common practice to use it on scrapes and cuts to fight infection. Otis shuddered and spoke for the first time. "That had to hurt some."

Coble shared a laugh with them. "Damned right it hurt. Like to peed-my-pants hurt."

Jake's expression sobered. "I see the star there on your shirt. I didn't get your name?"

He'd neglected that courtesy, and the man shouldn't have had to remind him. "Sorry. I'm Coble Bray." It pained him to see both men kind of set back and settle in their saddles. "I'm on my way to KC myself, but I'm in no hurry."

It was clear Jake would carry the conversation. Otis didn't say much. "Pleased to meet you, marshal. You the one they call The Deacon?"

Coble tipped back his hat and then stiff-armed Red away from his back. "Well, as you can imagine, I get called a lot of names. That's one of them.

Don't like it much." He grinned at them. "Don't worry...I won't preach at you.

"That's a mean horse you got there. I'd let him loose to run with the mustangs, was it me." Jake just shook his head. "Why do you keep him?"

Coble shrugged, appreciating the change of subject. "He's not too bad. Besides, he's the best trail horse I've ever had—go all day and night. Sometimes I need that in my line of work."

Both men were guarded, but still relaxed. As they started to leave, he spoke to them. "Boys, if you travel straight north from here, you're going to hit some small farms. They're mostly new sod busters up there, probably have unbranded cattle, and don't know they should be. Anyway, those mavericks would get kind of lost in that mixed herd of yours. The thing is, that meat will be life or death for them come winter. I'd consider it a favor if you go around. I wouldn't want to hear any complaints."

"Not exactly your jurisdiction, is it?" Jake gave him a hard look. "We don't take anything that belongs to someone else."

Coble held up a placating hand. "I didn't say it would be intentional."

"I'll pass the word on," Wheeler said, then seemed to consider a moment. "We might even have some calves we could drop off."

Calves were hard to deal with on any cattle drive. Usually, they died because they couldn't keep up or cluttered up the chuck wagon.

"I'm obliged, gentleman. If you're around the Cattleman's in KC, I'll buy the drinks."

He lost sight of them immediately in the trees and brush but could hear their progress for a few minutes. They were working north along the creek, looking for strays. It was nice to see some honest folks for once. The people he met in his line of work usually weren't. He gave Red a little nudge. Time to cross the creek and go find that beer.

Chapter Two

WIND RUSTLED THE TOPS OF THE PINE AND LIVE oak, gusting and swirling, rarely touching the forest floor below. Filtered light from a quarter-moon sifted through the swaying and twisting trees to cast mottled shadows on the path below.

The man who called himself The Watcher wasn't afraid of the dark. He loved it, molded to it, reveled in it to the point the darkness became part of him, and he of it. His nostrils flared with the smell of the forest—the cloying, honeysuckle-sweet odor mixed with decay and death, the freshness of running water through fern-choked streams. The sound of a rock rolling in the water meant a raccoon was probably fishing for crawdads in the shallow stream. Farther away, a single coyote tuning up its voice on a neighboring hill made him wonder, because coyotes didn't usually announce their presence in the spring. With no more sound than a passing ghost, he moved through the trees with a single-minded purpose, mumbling and talking to himself, chuckling at some joke only he could conjure.

He stopped suddenly and watched a fox as it trotted across his path, close enough to touch...it yelped and scooted away when he brushed his hand against its tail. The Watcher smiled. The fox headed toward where the raccoon fished. He was sure the fox would never dream of losing that fight but wouldn't stand a chance. If attacked, the raccoon pulls the fox into the water to drown it. He loved watching nature play out its little dramas. It was a gift, this love of the night.

Of course, he helped himself by wearing black clothes and gloves and smearing his face with black grease. Often at night, he'd stood by the trail when travelers went by. Once, he stood by as a band of Osage rode within a few feet of him. He was invisible. He loved it.

In the lee of a small bluff, a large boulder rested. Next to it and nearly under it, he moved aside a woven mat of vines. The vines stayed green because they were still attached to the roots and allowed to grow on the lattice-work of the mat. Dead vines would turn brown and give away the cave. With a satisfied grunt, he looked at the girl in the small opening.

The hunt for this girl was over, for now. Old Sheriff McGill had come close several times. But never close enough. It was time to move the prey to a safer place. Safer for him, not her. Oh, they'd looked hard, these sheep called townspeople, with their guns and horses, the burning torches that hid more than they revealed, shouting to each other all the time, shattering the natural quietness of the forest. He hated noise. They searched the fields around the town and searched the cabins and homes in the hills, stopping travelers, looking in wagons, but not in the right place. He chuckled to himself. Never in the right place. They just didn't know.

They couldn't *see*.

Shrouded in near darkness, the man extended his arms to the small girl crouched in the hollow in front of him.

"Come, child." He pulled the gag from her mouth. "It is time."

She shrank away from his voice, barely saw his hands reaching for her. "No. Please, no more. Please don't touch me. I don't want to go with you. Must I? Please let me go."

The question came so softly he had to strain to hear, had to separate the voices in his head from hers.

Finally... "Yes, child. You must."

The girl's voice was plaintive, shaking with weakness and fear. "Why?"

She was broken now, but by this time, they always were. He'd jerked her from her normal life while riding along a trail. It was a simple matter to knock her senseless, bind and gag her, and throw her into the cave. She had room to lie down, to sit, to stand if she could manage it, but the sides were wet and slick and afforded no way of escape. After a week of bread and water, and that was not too regular, she was weak and drained of spirit. Drained of hope. Compliant. They always were.

He paused a moment, gathering his thoughts, and shook his head to clear it. "It is written in the Bible."

"But why me?" Her hoarse voice gathered strength with mounting desperation. "Why choose me? I didn't do anything. I don't even know you."

"But child, I know you. I have watched you. You are a beautiful flower. And it is written in the Book that for a flower to be harvested, it first must wither, and then it must die."

"But I don't want to die." The girl sobbed. "My mother reads the Bible to me all the time. Little girls are never dying."

"No flower in the field yearns to be picked." He reached for her and helped her stand.

She looked around wildly, clearly seeking a way to escape, but she would see nothing but a dark shape hovering above her and more darkness beyond. And feel his strong grip. Always the squeezing, painful grip.

"Will it hurt?"

He stood, holding her up, listening to the weakness of her voice, the lack of will, and knew she was ready. The final step was acceptance. She'd been a strong girl, both in physical strength and spirit, and he'd hesitated to take her. As the voices told him it would, her spirit had left meals ago, helped along with the darkness and spiders in that musty hole.

"Of course there will be pain. The pain of living. The pain of being reborn." His kindly voice became impatient. "Don't waste your strength talking."

"But I am afraid, and-and my tummy hurts. I'm hungry." She was obviously stalling.

He realized the concept of time was something she'd never worried about before. Most people he'd seen never did, until it started running out, until they could see the end.

"The Christ cried out in pain."

"Can you give me water?" She tugged against his grip. "You never bring enough water."

"The Christ had thirst. He was given vinegar."

The girl tried to shrink away from the hands holding her, touching her, but he was too strong. "Please, don't do this to me."

"Come, child. My patience is at the end, and we have a long way to go. And look, you have soiled yourself. You must be cleansed. We must prepare you."

"Please don't hurt me." Her listless voice pleaded with him.

"But I must." He spoke as if the idea was perfectly logical and that she should understand.

"Please, I'll do anything, mister. Anything you want."

"You only have one thing to give. In the end, it is all we ever have to give."

"I don't understand." She sobbed.

"You cannot," he said with a shrug. How could she when he didn't understand it himself? Once again, the words echoed in his mind. *I must.*

She raised her face, trying to look directly into the horror of his eyes. "There will be more, won't there? To take my place?"

"You're a smart girl." He needed to make her understand. "There are many flowers in this place. All new. All beautiful. The harvest must continue." He lifted her by her shoulders, helping her to stand straight. "Your name will be written in the Book of Life."

The girl stood before him defiantly, even in her weakness, no longer trying to hide her nakedness. "You will pay for this. Someone will avenge me. Someone will come," she shouted angrily. "You will die for this. You will." She reached out suddenly and scratched his face, leaving a thin trickle of blood on his cheek.

The man looked at her a moment with his hand on his cheek, perplexed by her intensity and shocked by her spirit...and then smiled.

"I'll bet you've been praying for God to come and rescue you since I took you, and all you see is me. Have you prayed to God, that He would strike me down? How disappointing that must be for you."

"Someone will come."

He laughed softly as he pushed her toward the trail. "Who? Who will come, missy? No one will come for you. Not now. Not ever."

Chapter Three

The green hills were lush from early rains, the forest alive with the sounds and scents that come with spring. Water dripped from an aging linden tree onto the freshly turned earth, relentless in its journey, oblivious to the grief below.

Jessica Davis stood next to a wooden casket that held the body of her daughter—a daughter only twelve years old, once full of life and vitality. Always quick to help, to laugh...she moved her hand over the rough casket in a caressing move as if she were touching her daughter's hair, or back, or...she bit back a sob and steeled herself once again against the memory. This rough-hewn box just contained the shell of what Elaine had been. She knew her daughter's soul was in good hands. She knew...but still...

What do I do now? How can I believe in a God that would let this happen? She cried when her daughter went missing and cried during the frantic searching that had left her torn with despair. The tears were uncontrollable when gentle old Caleb McGill came home bringing Elaine's body, holding her with reverence and tenderness as he rode into the clearing in front of the cabin. He could have put her daughter in the back of a buckboard, but had chosen to carry the lifeless body in his arms, holding her to him as if to give comfort.

Now, Jessica was dry-eyed as she stepped back to allow her neighbors to finish burying her daughter. She knew these men well, their wives better. They were all so uncomfortable around her they wouldn't meet her eyes, and spoke in clipped sentences and monosyllables. Wives and children...afraid that whatever bad luck had stricken her would somehow rub off on them.

Jessica stood until all the well-wishers had shaken her hand, patted her shoulder, and murmured inane words of comfort. Words that held no meaning for her, offering comfort no one could give, quoting scripture of meaningless context from a God she'd begun to doubt.

———

CALEB MCGILL TURNED AWAY from the grave as the last hymn of the funeral service echoed through the hills...and his mind.

Amazing grace?

He had a hard time finding solace in God at a time like this. As he turned away, his ill-fitting store-bought suit coat opened just enough for the morning sun to glint lightly on the dull star pinned to his vest, a star that had seen years of use and the pain that went with the suffering and vagaries of man.

Behind him, the shuffling of feet and the soft murmurings of neighbors and friends filled the air, the clink of shovels scraping on rocks as men filled the grave. He turned to look over his shoulder at the woman who stood waiting for her young daughter to return to the earth. Jessica stood alone, she'd buried her husband just a year before.

The old sheriff shook his head. She should cry. She needs to cry, to let those square shoulders droop and be wrapped up in the arms of a good man.

As if she heard his thoughts, Jessica turned toward him, visibly seemed to gather her resolve around her like a cloak, and walked to him. Lifting the black lace veil, she took off her hat that revealed raven-black hair as her blue eyes pinned him on the spot, eyes that showed strain and grief, if you knew what to look for.

The strength of this woman. He waited, knowing what would come.

Under the drooping limbs of the linden tree, the same kind of tree their ancestors used in other countries as a place to administer justice, she came to ask the one question he didn't want to hear.

"Caleb." Her voice was soft yet firm. "Give me some good news for a change. Please, tell me you have an idea of who did this? And why."

"I'm sorry, Jessica. I just can't do it. Wish I

could. We combed these hills all of last week until dark and went out again at daybreak. I've had people talk to every bum and drifter we could find, checked every trapper camp and Indian hogan, and even rousted a few Gypsies I didn't know were around. We didn't find anything. I couldn't find a clue before she was found and have less of one now."

The woman stood in front of him, looking at him with purpose, strength, and no small amount of anger burning in her eyes. Her voice was so quiet he had to lean forward to hear.

"My Elaine is dead. People tell me you're one of the best lawmen in the country. I know you used to scout for the cavalry in Indian country. You're one of the most respected men around here. I've been told this by the very people you've put in jail, the people you deal with every day. Why, in God's name, can you not find something, some clue, to who did this? How can this be, Caleb?"

He slowly shifted his black hat from one hand to the other and then ran his fingers through graying hair. This was the moment he'd been dreading, and it was killing him. A lawman has to know why. The why of it is one of the driving forces behind what he does.

"Don't you think I've been trying? Good Lord, woman, I've been out every day. Vigilantes are running up and down the hills, and each group has already made up their minds just exactly who did this. Unfortunately, the choice they make is usually someone they have a grudge against. Now we have this bunch calling themselves the Baldknobbers moving in to clean all the riffraff out of the hills for us. If there was something to find, I gotta think someone would have stumbled on it."

He stood a moment in silence. "I guess I'm just not good enough, Jessica. I'm too old and too slow, and whoever did this is just too damned slick. This thing has got me buffaloed. It's not like anything I've seen before. Gunfights I can handle. Saloon fights and bank robberies I can handle. But this? I'd as soon be naked on the prairie in the middle of a Cheyenne war party than to be facing this."

Or her, right now.

"What about that? Do you think it was Indians?" Her voice was soft, plaintive.

"No, I don't. It just doesn't ring true. I know that's what everyone wants to think, what the town marshal is selling as true. But it's just too easy. A young girl like your Elaine?" Caleb shrugged. "They would steal her, maybe. Run off with her, or adopt her...maybe even sell her back to you. But kill her? Not likely."

———

JESSICA STOOD next to Sheriff McGill, lost in thought. She shook her head. It was the lack of closure that hurt the most. Not knowing why this happened or who murdered her daughter. If she let it, the hatred and despair would eat her up and kill her soul. Something had to be done.

She put her hand on the sheriff's arm to draw his attention back to her. "We've known each other a long time, Caleb. You know I'm not blaming you. After all, you've helped me many times. You helped me keep the ranch when my husband died, helped me find a job when I ran out of money. It is just..." Her voice faltered before finishing her thought. "I don't know what to do."

She watched the sheriff think about it a moment, and then his face settled into grim lines, his mind made up on something. "There's someone I can send for."

"Someone you know?" Hope soared in her voice and then died. "It's a little late now. But I still want to find who did this."

Slowly, as they talked, they drifted toward the small town nestled in the valley below. "The man I know is a deputy US marshal. Well, sort of. I think he's a special agent now. Anyway, he goes his own way. He'll come, if I ask."

"But what can he do that you can't? I figure you're the best tracker around."

"Well, it's a funny thing about that. Some men will read the prints in the trail, they keep their heads down, and every overturned rock and crushed leaf will lead them to the quarry. Others, like the Apache, look at the trail, think about the habits of who they are tracking, and go to the place the quarry has to be."

"And this man, what does he do?"

Caleb shook his head. "I've never seen the like. He does both. He's a hunter and a tracker...and, unfortunately for him, a killer."

"So? He hunts? What—wolves, mountain lions, bears? Tell me?" She sounded skeptical.

"People, Jessica." He looked directly at her. "He just hunts people. Last I heard, he was working for some judge out of Kansas City. Like I said, he's a deputy United States marshal, but not like any you hear of. They never send for him until a situation is damn near hopeless. Usually, that means some sheriff, like me, is killed trying to bring in somebody. When an outlaw is too good for a normal lawman to face, too fast with his gun, or has too many men around him, they call the Deacon."

"The Deacon? Like in a church?"

"No, it's just a nickname. His name is Coble Bray. Oh, he carries the Good Book and reads it. Although, I'd say he leans more toward the Old Testament. When you got sinners, he comes and reads to them from the Book, as the saying goes." Caleb glanced at her. "I mean it. Don't think he is some Bible pounder or circuit rider. He's a warrior, and no one brings him in to take prisoners."

"Then he sounds like the man we need. I don't want a prisoner." She looked up at him, eyebrows gathered in concern as she read the expression on his face. "Why don't you want his help?"

Finally... "I know him, and he's a good man. But he's got a wild streak. He's like an old buffalo bull.

Sometimes he's very unpredictable, and it doesn't take much to rile him up. Lately, from what I hear, people tend to die more often when he's around. That doesn't mean he kills without reason. It's just when a situation arises, he doesn't give many options."

"You send for him." She said it abruptly, with passion. "I'm sorry to be so selfish, and sorry if it causes a problem for you." She stood before him, fighting to keep her emotions under control, fighting the tears. "We've tried everything else. I just lost my daughter and don't know why. Somewhere, there's a man in these hills who needs killing. Send for this Deacon. And Caleb? You can tell him to leave his Bible at home."

Chapter Four

THE POKER GAME CONTINUED INTO THE DARK hours of the morning, longer than anyone intended. A progression of players had come and gone. The new players came, full of confidence and dreaming of doubling or tripling their pay, only to trudge away from the table with their pockets empty, bumming a drink or smoke, and dazed with the ruthlessness of the game and how quickly they'd lost their money.

The round table, nestled in the corner of the Cattleman's Saloon that had no windows, still held five players, the same players who'd started the game several hours before. Each of the remaining players slouched around the table in various stages of weariness, stubborn to the end—not to be outdone by the others, not to give in, and above all else, each determined not to lose.

Rancid and thick, a blue haze of smoke covered the room, hovering above the players' heads.

Anyone entering the room seemed to have the upper half of their body disappear right above the second button of their shirt. Their movements through the room barely stirred the cirrus layer. The acrid smell of cigars and stale beer assaulted the senses of all but the most hard-bitten and bleary-eyed...an acquired taste none wanted to learn.

A young man wearing a trainman's cap for the Kansas City Fort Scott & Gulf Railroad, red suspenders over a blue denim shirt, and a deep scowl on his face came in the door with military snappiness. Marching through the haze, avoiding tables and chairs, his polished lace-up boots shedding mud on the hardwood floor, he consulted with a bleary-eyed bartender who peeked under the noxious cloud and pointed toward the game in the corner of the room.

The trainman pushed his way through the assorted bar girls, worn-out ladies of the evening, and onlookers surrounding the table. If he'd been able to see clearly in the room, he would have immediately found the recipient of his message. The agent at the depot had given a good description —find a big man with wide shoulders, brown hair, a gray felt hat usually pulled low over his eyes, and, if playing poker, a big pile of chips in front of him. Coble Bray rarely lost.

"I have a telegraph for Mr. Bray. Mr. Coble Bray?" The trainman stood at the table expectantly, holding a piece of paper like it was an epistle from the mount.

Coble Bray tilted back his battered hat just enough for his eyes to take in the source of the new disturbance.

"He left, hours ago. Headed for Abilene on a twister called Satan. Hell of a horse." He cocked his head and looked toward the smoky ceiling. "You think it's going to rain in here? I swear I saw lightning a while ago."

The young trainman looked annoyed. "The lightning was outside, mister. The way it's raining, I'm going to start building my Ark. But I can't do that until I deliver this message. You want me to drown?"

Looking pointedly at the man who was ignoring him, he continued. "This is a priority message. It's been sent to every station up and down the line, and whoever delivers it gets a bonus."

"Sorry, son, never heard of him. Try some other saloon or the Rest In Peace Funeral Parlor, Barber Shop, and Bath House down the street. Seems like I heard he died from breathing too much smoke."

He folded four cards in a neat square and placed them on the table before him, placing the remaining discard carefully to the side. Because he'd been winning heavily, he kept all his movements slow, deliberate, and above the table. At this time and in this country, a man needed to be careful of his discards. As he rubbed his eyes, he thought of the hand he'd just placed on the table. The possibilities were few, a possible straight or a possible straight flush. Either hand would be a long shot, about fifty to one if he remembered right, but he played long shots every day.

Starting to call for his last card, the corpulent banker across the table interrupted him. Wearing a bowler hat, with mutton-chop sideburns framing his round, sweaty face, Franklin Sims sported an immense girth. The buttons of the banker's expensive vest strained to contain a huge belly that kept him at least three feet back from the table.

"He is stubborn, you know." Sims spoke to Coble with a sly grin. "I just happen to know this boy. I even know his pappy and brothers. They're all stubborn as mules. He'll just wait you out."

"Cut the crap and play the game." The surly voice came from a slick-looking man sitting next to the banker. He'd given his name as Charley, but anyone believing that would be a fool. He probably hadn't used his own name in so long he might not remember it himself. Two tied-down guns were conspicuous on his hips, and he spent an inordinate amount of time worrying about the angle of his hat and the knot of the blue silk scarf tied around his neck. He had the look of border ruffian written all over him, but he wasn't one of the *boys* from the Missouri/Arkansas line. Charley didn't look poor enough and was too much of a dandy.

At the abrupt outbreak from the gunman, one of the remaining players glanced around the table with a calm expression, raked in what little money he had left, and immediately threw in his cards, leaving the game. Making momentary eye contact with Coble, he cast a pointed look and wry smile over his shoulder at the young man with the guns and then strolled toward the bar. Acknowledging the contempt with a small nod, Coble slowly moved his left hand to his shirt pocket, extracting a long piece of peppermint, thinking that if anyone around the table were dangerous, it was the one heading for the bar. He was one of the boys from the border, Frank.

He broke the peppermint in half, holding on to one piece and depositing the other back in his pocket. Slate-gray eyes pinned Charley to his chair a moment, then he shifted his attention to the young trainman with the telegram.

"All right, son." He sighed, popping the piece of candy into his mouth like a cigar. "I'll take your message, but don't count on any bonus from the railroad. Never saw one yet that kept its word, and the KATY's no different."

Watching the exchange, Charley broke into the conversation again. "Mister, I said let's play. You've got most of my money on the table and I want a chance to get it back."

"I'd let it ride." The banker's voice interrupted Charley with a warning the young man ignored. Sims glanced around the table, taking in the wannabe gunman, another man in a business suit, and Coble Bray. "I am sure we can wait until this man reads his message. It's probably important. We don't need any unpleasantness in a friendly game of poker now, do we?"

Carefully laying the telegram face down on the table, thinking about the banker's comment, he nudged his hat up a fraction, shifted the peppermint stick to the other side of his mouth, and picked up his cards. On one point, he disagreed. Poker was never friendly.

"It's not a problem, Mr. Sims." Then, directing his calm attention to Charley, he said. "All right, I'll take one card."

Charley tried to stare him down, then gave up and dropped his gaze to the table. With a sneer, he flipped him a card.

Placing the card face down on the telegram without looking at it, he estimated the money in Charley's pile across the table and then pushed a like amount of his own money into the center.

"Wait a minute."

He glanced at the other man at the table, someone he'd been unaccountably curious about for some time. The player who'd spoken was a man with delicate features who'd given the name Sandy and rarely spoke during the game, a man who played steady and careful. He was also a man who had the softest eyes he'd ever seen. Not a big winner in the game, but seemed to have an uncanny knack for avoiding any large losses. As he watched, the man folded his cards into a neat little pile.

"I fold," Sandy spoke quietly.

The banker threw in his cards. "Me, too."

"I'm sorry, Mr. Sims...and, Sandy, is it? My apologies for the lack of manners." Coble met the gaze of both. "I did jump the gun a little. With your permission?"

Sandy nodded a cool assent.

"All right, then." Coble turned his attention back to Charley. "One shot takes it all, son. Short and sweet. I'll see whatever you have in your meager little stack."

"Mister, you haven't even looked at your hole card. And quit calling me son. You ain't my daddy."

He smiled at the man. "Well, thank God for small favors. I'll play these. What will it be?"

"Hell. You're bluffing and we both know it." Charley shoved his remaining money to the center of the table, along with jacks and kings, with a deuce kicker. "Two pair, which has got to be more than you've got with that busted flush you've been holding."

Coble turned over his last card, an eight of hearts, filling the bottom end of his straight flush, then grinned again at the man across the table. "Well, look at that, fifty to one."

Stunned for a moment, Charley erupted from the table with an oath, chair skidding across the floor behind him. Amid the silence of sucked-in breaths and shocked glances, his hands streaked for the pearl-handled revolvers holstered at his side.

And stopped.

For just a moment, Coble felt sorry for the man. The gun Charley saw pointed at him wasn't pretty.

It was old and scarred, blackened by powder smoke on the end, smooth where it mattered, and he was sure the barrel looked bigger than any cave opening Charley had ever seen. When he finally looked up from the Navy Colt pointed at him, Charley's expression was one of dread. For a second, he seemed to tense in expectation of a bullet.

"What's your last name, Charley?"

"Uh...Joiner."

He looked at him for a long minute, searching his memory. "Do I know you?"

The man was actually dripping sweat on the floor. "No."

"Then why all this stupid gunplay?" Coble yelled at him, causing the man to flinch backward. Behind him, there was the distinct sound of glasses falling, along with the soft cursing of the bartender.

Then, in a quiet voice that made everyone lean forward a little, he spoke to the would-be gunman. "Well, Mr. Uh...Joiner, I'd like to give you some advice. It might save your life. Probably won't, but you're going to get it anyway. You're slow, son. You have no coordination and not an ounce of judgment. You have the hands of a child. You're weak. I don't see one callus on your palms and I doubt if you've done an honest day of work in your life. If you're looking to make a living with those fancy guns you're so fond of, which are too big for your hands by the way, you are in the wrong line of work. My advice? Take them off. They'll just buy you a fast ticket to Boot Hill."

Coble paused and looked at the hapless man a moment, then patted his shirt pocket, looking for that last piece of peppermint he'd stashed away. After he found it, he addressed Charley again.

"Tell you what. Why don't you sit back down real quiet, and maybe I will forget you are here."

As he finished speaking, he glanced at Sandy, sitting next to the banker. Small but sturdy-looking, reddish brown hair tied back with a piece of rawhide string, the man watched him steadily with a barely concealed look of feverish excitement in his eyes. He noticed the man's right hand rested slightly inside his open coat, and he could tell by the tension in the wrist, the fingers were splayed wide. A knife or a short gun in a shoulder holster?

Coble's gun barrel moved a fraction of an inch and the man instantly brought his hand back into view. A message sent and understood, needing no further lines of communication.

A grinning range hand, bow-legged and rough, brought back Charley's chair. "Hey, gunfighter. Next time, take the hammer thong off those shooters. You might do better."

Stunned at his mistake, Charley's hands moved toward the loops covering the hammers of his guns.

"Well, not now, you idiot." The range hand laughed.

Lifting his hands like they were burned, Charley stared around the table a moment before he gingerly sat down, not knowing how this would play out and especially having trouble figuring out what to do with his hands.

Coble heard the range hand comment to one of his friends. "I think he peed his pants."

"Mister?" The stubborn young trainman hadn't moved an inch, even during the near gun play.

"What?" Coble said with exasperation.

"I think you should read the telegram. I need to send back an ask...uh...ax...uh, aw hell. I need to tell them you got the message and where to send my money."

"What's your name, son?"

The young man hesitated a moment. "Bonney. William Bonney."

Coble's eyebrows went up. "Katy McCarty's boy?"

The man rolled his eyes. "Not hardly."

"I suppose they call you Billy?"

"Me and about a dozen others. Might as well be Smith or Gomez, there are that many of us around."

He studied the young trainman a moment as he picked up the telegram with his left hand.

"Well, Mr. Bonney, the word you're looking for is *acknowledgment*. It's a big word that means what you just said. Some professor with nothing better to do probably made the word up to impress a girl, so I wouldn't use it either."

He turned his attention to the telegram.

APRIL 19, 1878

TO: SPECIAL AGENT COBLE BRAY

MORE TROUBLE THAN I CAN HANDLE. NEED
YOU. CALEB

For a fleeting moment, he was lost in thought.
Caleb McGill worked as a sheriff in a little town just
south of the Arkansas border. Years ago, the old
scout had given him a home after he escaped from
an Apache camp and then took him to raise. His
pulse quickened as he thought of the man who was
like a father to him, who'd taught him everything he
knew.

A tough old man, and if Caleb's in trouble...

With a sibilant whisper, his Colt slipped back
into its holster. To knowing onlookers, the plain
walnut grips, sweat-stained and dark, spelled
constant use and care. The holster, well-oiled, hard,
and smooth, would never slow down a draw. To
people who didn't know him, the gun symbolized
who he was and what he did. But to him, the gun
was a tool and nothing more.

Raising a cold, expressionless gaze to meet those
of the players sitting across from him, he spoke
softly. "Gentlemen, if you'll excuse me? I have business to attend to. It's been a pleasure."

He pushed his winnings to the middle of the
table and made eye contact with a man at the bar,
who responded with a slight nod. Going out the
door with the young trainman in tow, Coble said,
"I'll meet you at the train station, Billy. Figure on a
horse car and engine rolling to Joplin. Give me an
hour or so. I have a couple of errands first."

Waiting on the front walk of the saloon, the man who'd left the game early and stayed at the bar spoke to him. "Why didn't you shoot that peckerwood?"

"Hell, Frank, he's just a kid. Wouldn't be worth the trouble." They came together and shook hands.

Frank shook his head and laughed. "That one's too stupid to live, I'm thinkin'. You need something from me?"

"I'm heading down to Big Springs, Frank. The one just across the Arkansas line. I just don't want any misunderstandings." He smiled as he spoke.

"What's up? Judge sending you out after border jumpers now?"

"No, nothing like that. I don't really care what you boys are up to. I just got a message from Caleb. Says he has trouble he can't handle. It's hard to imagine what that would be."

When Frank nodded his head in agreement, Coble asked, "Do you know Big Springs? Have you heard anything from down there?"

Frank grinned and nodded again. "I know it well enough to leave it alone. Caleb would shoot us full of holes if we bothered his town."

"Well, if you get a chance, do me a favor. Let people know I'm coming. I don't want a reception committee."

"We're just peaceful farmers. That's all."

Coble's voice was sarcastic. "Yeah, with thousand-dollar pigs. Just put out the word. Look. I'm not judging you, either way. I'm not looking for trouble."

"Sure. Okay. If you're traveling fast, you may beat me home, but I'll do my best."

"That's all I ask. And Frank? You do remember I keep my money in Sims' bank?"

"What?" Frank said innocently, drawing the word out. "Why, who do you think you're talking to? Besides, I didn't even know this town had a bank."

"Frank, some men chase women. Others will chase whiskey. I know you. The first place you ride by when you come to any town is the bank. How many guards does this one have?"

"Well, we all got our weaknesses, and I counted four guards." Frank grinned. "What's your weakness, Coble?"

"Outlaws with sad stories." As he walked away, he raised his hand and waggled all his fingers, saying over his shoulder. "Five. Five guards."

AFTER COBLE BRAY left the saloon, Charley Joiner struggled a moment, trying to clear his throat so he could speak. His voice came out in a rough, high-pitched squeak. "Who the hell is that man?"

Sims chuckled softly. "I tried to warn you, but you weren't listening. He's a regular here. You know, this may be as close as you'll ever come to being killed without taking lead."

"So, who?"

Sandy, still sitting on the other side of the gunman, grinned. "I believe the gentleman is Coble Bray. He's a federal marshal. Sort of."

"Hell, that name don't mean nuthin' to me."

"Then I assume you've heard of The Deacon?"

The young man blanched and looked like he was going to upchuck his supper and beer.

The banker turned his gaze directly on the gunman. "You're lucky to be alive, young man. The marshal's very quick on the shoot. Maybe too quick for some tastes."

Charley slumped back in his chair, suddenly wet with cold sweat. "Jesus. I heard about him. He killed four men in that fight out in Kansas just a couple of weeks ago. They had him boxed, and when they braced him, he just took them down." Unsteadily, he got up and walked toward the bar. "Jesus."

Standing, straightening his coat, Sandy spoke to the banker. "Seems like Mr. Uh...Joiner just found religion. Mr. Bray left his winnings. What are we supposed to do with that?"

"The marshal always leaves his poker winnings," Sims said. "The bank keeps a Widow and Orphans fund. That's where he wants it."

"I wouldn't have expected such charity from a man like that."

"He's an odd one, all right. From what little I know of him, he's the definition of the word gentleman. As the saying goes, *he's an enigma inside an enigma*. To my knowledge, there's not a better or kinder man anywhere. Trouble is, there's a crazy streak in him. Something happens to him in a fight. Well, you just witnessed it tonight. I saw eyes like that once on a sharpshooter who worked for General Sherman during the war. When he needs to...he just turns everything off. I guess that's why Marshal Bray's always sent to bring in the bad ones, the real hard cases."

The banker paused a moment, looking at the other man. "I didn't get your last name?"

"That's right," Sandy said. "You didn't."

The banker turned away, smiling, not in the least offended, and watched Charley as the gunman progressed to the bar. The bartender gave Charley a drink and, with a sympathetic look, waved off the two bits offered.

Sighing to himself, the banker picked up the telegram, started to crumple it to throw it away, hesitated a moment, and then read it. His eyebrows first raised in surprise, then pinched together in concentration. He knew Caleb McGill, knew the life he had led before retiring to a sheriff's job in a sleepy little town in the Arkansas hills. Caleb was tough as leather, and no border jumper in his right mind would brace him.

What kind of trouble could he have that he'd send for Coble Bray?

He shrugged. It won't matter. With Caleb McGill and Coble Bray in the same place, there won't be a hardcase for miles who isn't running for his life, or shot to ragdolls.

He bent forward and gathered the money from the table. It was another good day for the orphans. The widows could always take care of themselves. The saloon was full of them.

As he walked from the room, he heard a range hand say, "He did. I saw it. He peed his pants."

A sarcastic reply followed. "You would'a done it too if the Deacon had pointed his shooter at you."

Chapter Five

SANDY WAITED FOR THE BANKER TO COME OUT OF the front door. "If I need to speak to the marshal, where do you think I could find him?"

Sims spoke as he walked by. "Church."

"Church?"

"He always goes to church before he goes out on a job."

Sandy stood, squinting into the early morning sun, trying to burn off the fog and drizzle of the storm the night before.

Church. Huh. Staring distastefully at the cigarillo burning in his hand, he flipped it away with a look of disgust and walked down the street, boot heels clicking softly on the boardwalk. Turning down a narrow passage between two buildings, he retrieved the horse left tied at the back, taking a moment to tighten the cinches. He hadn't intended to be gone so long, or he'd have taken the saddle off.

A two-mile ride brought him to a small campsite

situated close to a fast-moving stream, hidden from any scrutiny by a thick stand of red cedar.

Swinging down from the horse, he stood a moment, stretching out the kinks brought on by sitting for hours in a straight-backed saloon chair. Then, with a quick headshake, the hat swept off, and a mass of black hair tumbled out and around, framing the face and transforming it into an altogether different look. Kneeling at the stream, a copious amount of water made the dark facial tan disappear, along with the small, black mustache.

Standing, with the transformation complete, she resisted the desire to strip and dive into the water. She felt that dirty. But with the town so close, she didn't want to chance some roving cowboy stumbling across her campsite. She smiled. Maybe later. I've had enough excitement for one day.

Maria Santos, or Sandy, settled for wetting her neckerchief and bathing around her shoulders and neck. Reaching under her shirt, she untied the strap binging her chest and took a huge breath of relief, gently massaging herself. It wasn't easy to conceal what nature had generously given her.

For a moment, her eyes focused on something far away, with totally female thoughts and a half-smile forming on her lips...thinking of Coble Bray.

Now *there* was a man!

He puzzled her. By all accounts, a killer. Smart. Relentless. Thought by some to be the best tracker in the country, but about that, she didn't agree. Her

father was the best tracker. Of course, some preju-
dice might be involved there.

She'd heard from her father all about Coble Bray.
The Deacon.

How could that name inspire fear in men? It
sounded religious. She'd heard he was stone cold,
fearless, and ruthless. Yet today, he'd spared a man
he could have easily killed and no one would have
blamed him. Then, learning that the considerable
amount of poker winnings left on the table went to
the widows and orphans fund had impressed her.

Of course, that wasn't the most unsettling fact.
For some unaccountable reason, she got warm all
over just looking at him. She'd looked into his eyes
and they were not cold.

One of the reasons she'd come west was to see
the man her father talked about so much. The other
reason had to be held a little closer to the vest.
She'd heard the country she was going into was
fatally hard on Pinkerton agents.

She turned and pulled a small tally book from
her pack. Flipping through the pages, she came to a
blank spot and started writing. She stopped, absent-
mindedly chewing on the pencil and loosening the
belt of her pants, thinking about the poker game.

It had been close, and a couple of times, she
thought he would see through her deception. None
of the others had. She'd realized her mistake the
moment she sat in on the game and glanced around
the table. The smoothness of her hands had given
her away, a mistake she vowed not to make in the

future. She'd seen Bray glance at her hands when she dealt cards and once again during play. More than once, she'd caught him looking at her eyes, not her face. That unsettled her because, in this day and time, that kind of personal scrutiny was an insult.

Thinking of the players, and of her mission, she ran them through her mind. The banker she discounted. He was surely just as he appeared. From the looks of him, he'd not been on a horse in years.

Charley Uh Joiner—she smiled at that—was a bad man looking for a place to happen. But not wanted yet. In her opinion, he would drop his gun going into a bank before he could ever rob it.

The man who'd thrown in his cards and left the game. He was a possible. She was sure there was a gun hanging from a lanyard around his neck, concealed beneath his shirt. He was a possible, and her employer paid well for *possibles*. Unfortunately, she didn't know the man's name.

She shook her head, amazed at herself. She'd never dreamed working for the Pinkertons would be like this. Although she feared discovery by the various gangs of outlaws operating along the Missouri-Arkansas border, her greatest fear was Pete finding out. Pete Santos was under the impression his daughter had been going to a nice, peaceful finishing school back east.

Her plan was to hop the train down to Mindenmines, then on to Joplin. Pete was to meet her there with horses. What they did after that depended on Pete. He was a good father. She just wasn't sure how he was going to take her news about not being in the finishing school and the job she had.

———

COBLE BRAY WALKED SLOWLY down the narrow aisle toward the altar in the old church, a building that used to be outside the city, but the railroad and growing population had expanded the borders of the town to include it. The sound of his boots echoed on the wooden floor and rough-hewn logs that made the walls, announcing his presence to any and all. Sunlight filtered through the side windows of multicolored cut glass, showering the neat rows of weathered pews with dusty light.

He fought a sneeze and his right hand strayed to the raised end of each pew as he passed, savoring the feel of the polished wood. Like the hymnals they held, the benches were seasoned and worn, made with loving care, and each alike as ripples in a pool of water. He could smell the linseed oil used to preserve the wood and bring out the grain, imagined he could feel it on his fingers. Most of all, the wood was solid and steady, quiet in its strength, offering refuge and rest to all who came. He envied the artisans who could make things like this out of wood.

Silently, his eyes drawn to the simple cross carved from oak on the wall behind the altar, he moved forward. He dropped his hat on the first pew, closest to the altar. The one bench few people ever polished with their Sunday best. He knew a church always fills from the back to the front and felt an affinity to the common man who never wanted to get too close to the fire and brimstone message coming from the pulpit.

He stopped at the two steps leading to the raised dais of the altar. Holding a hand to his left side, he grimaced as he went first to one knee, then the other. Finally, in stages, he relaxed in the quiet confines of the church and began to pray.

———

A DOOR to the side of the altar opened quietly, and a robed man stood for a moment, watching Coble, the only man he'd ever seen who seemed to kneel at attention.

He watched, and even with his eyes closed, the kneeling man had all the presence of a sleeping lion. Or one of King Henry's knights—massive sword driven into the ground, the handle being a cross that never leaves his side, guiding his way. Only, in this case, the sword his friend carried was a Navy Colt.

After a moment, he walked quietly down the steps and sat in the first pew. He gently chided himself for putting on his vestments and robe, when there was no service to attend to. But deep down, he knew it was a sign of respect and could do no less in front of this man. He picked up the brown, nondescript hat and wondered at the silver band around it and how it defined the man who wore it. Just a hat, plain as day and nothing special, but with a silver band to glint in the sun and say to all, *Here I am*. Silently, not wanting to interrupt, he waited.

———

COBLE STOOD, swayed a moment, and then caught his balance. Looking down at his hand, he saw a small spot of blood, which he quickly wiped on his pants. The bullet meant to kill him had left a grazing flesh wound. A matter of a couple of inches and a difference of angle, and he'd be dead. But that's how he lived.

A couple of inches away.

He turned and walked to the pew, reaching out for his hat as he acknowledged the preacher with a nod.

"Where are you off to this time?"

He looked askance at the preacher. "You can tell I'm going somewhere?"

The man in the long robe and vestments looked at him a moment and then shrugged. "You never come to Sunday service, and yet here you are on a weekday. And you always come in and pray before you go out on a job. Strangely enough, you seem to want forgiveness not for what you have done...but for what you're about to do. It's an easy assumption to make that you're going out on a job."

He shook his head, smiling ruefully. "I'll have to watch out. In my line of work, being predictable isn't a good idea. Besides, I don't pray for redemption. I'm afraid that horse has already left the barn." He smiled at the pastor. "Perhaps I pray because I need all the help I can get."

The pastor gave a small chuckle. "I think, in this case, you can take the chance on being predictable. No harm will come to anyone in this house."

Coble smiled grimly. "Don't be too sure. A man can die in this house as well as any other, though we protect it with our lives."

As he sat in the pew across the aisle from the preacher, he handed across the telegram and a worn envelope. "Here's the letter you forwarded to me. It's from a Mrs. Davis, whose daughter has been killed. It's a wonder the letter caught up with me. I wasn't going to go. It's been two weeks. That's a long time and a very cold trail...I just didn't figure any good would come from it. Now I received one from Caleb. I can't imagine him needing help."

The pastor spoke softly as he took the papers. "There's nothing new about someone being killed in this country. There are still Indian renegades, white renegades still reliving the war, or just plain outlaws. Evil is everywhere. What's different about this?"

"Caleb's message. It just says, *need help. Come a'runnin'*. I can't remember him ever asking for help."

The pastor gazed out a side window, lost in thought a moment. "Strange, the lack of details. How far away?"

"Not far. Just down to Big Springs, Arkansas. Across the line."

The pastor shrugged. "Then it's a simple decision. One you've already made, I'm sure. You must go. A friend calls."

He glanced at the enigma that was Pastor A. Schuler. His first name was August, but he'd never heard anyone use it. The pastor was a short, sturdy man with iron-gray hair and steely-blue eyes. But there was compassion there, and understanding. Best of all, an understanding of him. He often wondered about that. Maybe that defined a friend—someone who knows you well and still tolerates you.

"I see you still have that silver band on your hat."

"Priest, you should know better than mess with a man's hat," he grumbled, rolling the brim and checking the crease. His gaze settled on the hatband. "It will likely get me killed someday, the way it reflects light. Still..." He smiled. "It was a gift from my wife. I like it."

"Coble, I've asked you—please do not call me Priest. I'm a Lutheran pastor. There's a difference."

He glanced thoughtfully at the pastor a moment and then settled his hat on his head. "Well, you've told me lots of things, Priest." He paused in thought. "I come here and pray. I talk to you and tell you all my troubles." He gave the pastor an amused look. "All of which seems a whole lot like confession to me. But nothing changes when I pray, Priest. Why is that? My knees still hurt. My back hurts. The hole in my side hurts. And I still don't have answers."

"Maybe you're asking the wrong questions. You're still alive, and there are some terrible, terrible men who aren't dealing out their brand of evil anymore. Isn't that enough of an answer?"

"You make me out to be some sort of avenging angel. I'm not. My own death is just a matter of time. Skill and luck can only take a man so far."

"Then take off that star if you have so many doubts." The pastor reached out and touched the worn walnut handle of the Colt. "Put up this gun."

He involuntarily touched the star on his shirt and then let his hand return to his side. It's the simple questions that have no good answers. "You know I cannot."

"Then," said Schuler softly, "that's your answer, and you must learn to live with it. You cannot change what you are, no more than a beaver in a stream can change its habits. If you read your Bible and take the trouble to count, you'll find a lot more warriors who do God's work than prophets and priests."

"And which are you? A warrior, prophet, or priest?" He'd known Schuler a few years now. It was a fair question.

Schuler smiled. "I'm just a pastor of a small country church."

"Yeah." Coble grimaced. "And I'm the Queen of England."

The pastor pointed to the bloodstain on Coble's

side, deftly changing the subject. "So, tell me how you got this wound you're trying so hard to ignore."

"Not much to tell. I went out toward Wichita to see a couple of men. I found them in a little two-by-twice settlement that didn't even have a name. The two men turned into four, and we had a short and very loud discussion in the corral behind the stable."

Schuler shook his head. "Four men, and you doubt God's help?"

Coble chuckled grimly. "It did seem as if I had a lot of luck on this one. It was an ambush, pure and simple. But they were in so much of a hurry to kill me they got in each other's way. And don't be mourning for their souls, Priest. I asked them to come in peacefully. Seems like they had other ideas."

———

THE CONVERSATION BROUGHT BACK small vignettes in Coble's mind. The gusting wind that ruffled his hair and dried the sweat on his brow as he took off his hat and studied the men. The corral smelled of decay, old and new, and a couple of horses stirred the dust as they moved toward a water trough to his left. It was fitting. There will be more compost to build up the soil after this day was done.

Latigo Johnson and his brother Frederick waited for him at the corral. He'd spoken to them earlier about the warrant and they said they needed to get their horses. It was a minor *failure to appear*, nothing serious.

Both stood alike with one foot on the bottom corral post, a posed study of nonchalance. They were working so hard to look at ease, Coble knew immediately that he'd walked into a trap.

Would it be today, that magic bullet with his name on it?

A glint of reflected sunlight winked from the door of the loft on his left, and he drew his gun. His memory was of gunshots, powder smoke, and horses milling in the corral, panicked by the explosion of sound. The man in the loft pitched headlong to the ground as the two by the corral tried to draw their weapons.

They were startled. They'd expected some talk, setting him up for a shot in the back from their hidden assassin. The surprise gone, the outlaws went for their guns. In his haste, Latigo fired his first shot into the ground and took a slug in the belly for it. Frederick caught his spur on the corral post as he turned to fire and never got off a shot. A bullet ricocheted off a post next to him, filling his gun hand with slivers of wood. A second notched the second button down from his shirt collar.

Coble was firing at them when a bullet cut across his side. The powder smoke cleared with a sudden gust of wind, and he faced the fourth man whose name he never knew.

Smiling, the man took slow and careful aim, like he was at target practice. Coble flipped his gun up and fired. The first bullet caught the man in the belly, bending him over in a macabre bow. The second blew away the shocked expression on his face. The man had been too sure of himself. Too sure he had an edge. Too slow. Too arrogant. In the space of a couple of minutes, four men were dead and Coble was walking to his horse, blood running down his side. Automatically, he reloaded his pistols. He didn't remember pulling the second gun.

Staying long enough to get their names, he headed back toward Kansas City.

Latigo Johnson and his brother Frederick, along with Mike Foss and Irish Jimmy O'Neal, could be taken off the rolls.

———

COBLE CLEARED his trip down memory lane as they both stood to leave the church. He said to Pastor Schuler, "People tell me I can't serve two masters, that I cannot have a gun in one hand and a Bible in another."

"And yet, here you stand. I have never seen a more faithful servant. Those people you speak of, your detractors, never read the Old Testament, or a good part of the New. Don't give up your Bible just because you carry a gun. When good men give up their guns, we'll have anarchy and chaos."

Coble sighed in exasperation. "I can't get past the premeditation, Priest. The difference in taking life, either accidental, self-defense, or by war...and murder...is premeditation. The Bible says we shall not commit murder, and murder is defined by premeditation. Yet, when I go after a man to bring in, I know he may fight. In fact, most of them do. If he chooses to fight, I know I'll kill him."

"And yet, he has his chance. I know that about you." Schuler thought for a moment. "Coble, don't confuse premeditation with predestination."

He stared at the pastor for a few seconds and then grunted. "Great. More riddles."

"Not riddles." The pastor smiled benignly at him. "Clarity. You know, I haven't always been a preacher."

He looked at Pastor Schuler, at the cold blue eyes and hard face, and said seriously, "What a surprise."

Chapter Six

THE EARLY AFTERNOON SUN WAS TOO HOT FOR THE month of April as Coble stepped off the train at a water stop on the north side of Joplin, Missouri. He'd boarded the Kansas City Fort Scott & Gulf just south of Kansas City, rode it all the way to Baxter Springs, Kansas, then boarded the Short Creek and Joplin track that brought him east into Webb City. Glancing around at the gray and wind-battered buildings, his gaze found a man leading horses toward him.

Pete Santos walked on wrangler's legs so bowed from decades of riding that he couldn't stop a three-hundred-pound boar from running between them. His wrinkled skin hung on a battered frame of loosely connected bones that rattled and creaked as his boots sent up little puffballs of dust from the street. A wide grin split his wrinkled face as he shook Coble's hand.

"Figured this was where you'd show up."

"How're ya doin', Pete?" His grin matched that of the old cowpuncher. Pete preened a moment. "Gettin' better lookin' every day."

"I can see that. Hell, you don't look a day over a hundred. Any place to get a beer around here?"

The man nodded. "Yeah, but it tastes like coal dust."

"Well, trot it out. I'm drier than cactus toes. I see you got old Red out of the cattle car."

"I don't see why you like that horse. He bites, he stomps, and has the disposition of a rattler. He even scares the mules."

He chuckled. "He always gets me where I'm going. You ready to explain all this to me?"

"Yeah, I can do that. Say, I heard you took some lead. You're moving around pretty good."

He nodded soberly. "It was just a graze, but it was close."

Pete suddenly became serious. "I'll lay this whole thing out for you, but you better wet your whistle first. It'll go down a lot easier."

———

AN HOUR later found them both standing on the ramshackle porch of the combination mercantile, barbershop, restaurant, and saloon. Pete had just finished telling him what he knew about Caleb's trouble at Big Springs.

"So, just how old was this girl?" Coble asked again, still trying to get his head around it.

Pete thought a moment. "Eleven or twelve."

He nodded, lost in thought a moment. "Young."

"What are you thinkin'?"

"It just doesn't seem right. Nobody bothers a girl that young. Do you remember how the Indians used to sell young girls to the French for the slave trade? I hear there's still a market for that down New Orleans way. Probably always will be. Maybe somebody tried to snatch her and she got killed."

Pete shook his head. "That slave trade was twenty, maybe thirty years ago. Now back east something like that could happen. There are so many people, when someone disappears, they ain't missed too much. Out here, that ain't the case. Besides, western men are almighty particular about how their women-folk are treated, especially children. It'd be too risky for anyone to try that."

"Maybe so." He grinned. "Of course, most people aren't nearly as smart as you are. Someone may not know all the hidden rules of western lore and protocol. Obviously, something happened to her."

"There you go, using them big words again. And let's just hope you're smart too. Me? I'm stumped. After I talked to Caleb, I don't want to go over there." Pete paused. "This has about killed Caleb. I hadn't seen him for a while. Looks like he's aged twenty years, and he don't have it to give."

"You want out?"

"Naw. You know I'm just talkin'. I ain't left you hangin' yet."

He thought a moment. "I'd like you to head on back, Pete. I'll travel slow enough to let you get ahead of me. Once I get to Big Springs, I'll find you."

Pete could find out a lot because he wasn't known in Big Springs. As soon as Coble hit town, everyone would know of it.

Pete nodded. "I'll leave word with McGill if I'm not there. I've got to pick up someone first."

He raised his eyebrows. "Need help? I can watch your back."

"No. I'm meeting someone. A relative. Although watching my back might not be a bad idea."

"I didn't know you had any relatives." He gazed at his friend with wonderment. This was new information.

"Sure I do. Ya think I sprung from a rock?"

Grinning at the irascible old puncher, he just shook his head. He would never weasel the truth out of Pete. Not unless Pete wanted to tell it.

Pete finally broke the silence. "How long will you be?"

"Gimme a week. I'll be in. Why? If that girl's already dead, we're not in too big a hurry, are we? What's the rush?"

"I don't know. Like I said, this whole thing has me spooked. I cain't see Indians doing this, but there's a measure of people who want to lay this thing at their feet. The trouble is, the border country's full of riff-raff, bank robbers, and a bunch of vigilante artists called Baldknobbers. Half of them are looking to hang the other half. No tellin' what you'll run into."

"Doesn't matter." He searched for a peppermint. "Whoever would kill a young girl, I have a personal interest in meetin' up with. I don't care what their pedigree is."

Pete looked askance at him a moment. "Dammit, why don't you suck on a cigar like a grown man?"

———

COBLE REINED in his sorrel gelding at the top of a bluff next to a lightning-blasted pine that looked to twist in the agony of life. The horse never forgave mankind for the cutting that made him a gelding, and old Red took the opportunity to turn and try to nip his leg. Avoiding Red's teeth without even thinking about it, he scanned the White River bottoms below. There was a story in this country ahead of him. A story of a murdered girl and a killer not caught, of an old friend asking for help, and a letter from a young, angry mother that burned in his shirt pocket. The letter was worn and creased because it demanded to be read, and he did it often. The letter begged for immediate action. And he was weeks late.

He would never have skylined himself on this bald and burned-off bluff if he was in Kansas or farther west, but this was settled country on the Missouri and Arkansas border, and the day's heat made him irritable. If someone wanted to bring him trouble today, they'd get a belly full.

He took off his brown, low-crowned hat and wiped the sweatband with his bandanna as he looked at the country ahead of him. In the distance, shadows from the clouds marched across the hills and valleys with stretches of bright sunlight peppered in between. Closer in, the sun was blocked out by the black clouds behind him, punctuated by flashes of lightning and rumbles of thunder.

Another glance below fixed the position of the ranch house and barn that could barely be seen through the trees. Farther off to the east, several thin columns of smoke rose, and he guessed that would be the location of Big Springs.

The gray and white thunderheads had rolled up behind him all morning, and the first cold drops of rain fell. The drops were huge and widely spaced, like unfrozen hailstones and sounded like an egg dropping when they hit the ground. Gusty wind moaned through the oak and hickory, pushing cold air on the back of his neck. The temperature would drop dramatically in a few moments. Glancing down the talus slope before him, he knew there wouldn't be time to stop and put on his slicker or try and traverse the dangerous slope before the onslaught hit and made it too unsafe for passage. There wasn't time for both.

Clamping his hat tighter on his head, he eased Red down the side of the mountain in a zigzag pattern, scattering mud and shale and leaving a shifting trail behind them. Red was a flat country horse and didn't like the mountains and hills. He was sure the horse would show his disapproval soon enough.

After traversing the shale and finding solid ground at the bottom, he reined the horse to a stop. He started to reach behind him for his slicker, but the sky opened with a clap of thunder, scattering smoking wood chips from the old tree above. Lightning once again assaulted the beleaguered pine and blew bark and small limbs into the air.

Already wet, he kneed Red under the towering oak and shorter dogwood that grew under the canopy of the taller trees. Honeysuckle and sumac grew in dappled light penetrating the higher cover. He was just thankful the leaves were thick enough to reduce the rain to a tolerable drizzle. Finally, deciding he couldn't get any more wet or cold, he turned the horse into a ghost of a trail that led around a huge, moss-covered boulder and into the clearing of the ranch house he'd seen from above.

He rode around a sturdy barn of rough-hewn lumber that had the gaps between the logs closed with mortar. The barn was finely built so there were precious few of those. The pole corral, situated against the hillside, was tightly constructed and sturdy. His entry into this small glade was silent as his horse trod on short grass growing on rocky ground, any noise of their progress muffled by the rain.

If a horse could cuss, Red was doing it. Wet, tired, and covered in mud, he snorted and blew, showing his indignation at the world in general. Coble sharply heeled him in the flank, but the deed was done.

Four startled men jerked around to face him when he rode into view. Three sat their horses, and the fourth stood close by, one foot raised like he was afraid to put it down.

A tall, slim woman in a simple print dress stood on the porch of her home. Her long, dark hair fell past her shoulders and was held back on one side by a silver comb that glinted in the subdued light. Her face bore a grim expression, and the shotgun she held didn't offer much hospitality. Both hammers of the old Greener shotgun were locked back and ready.

He took in the situation instantly, at least all he needed to know, and approved her choice of the shotgun for a weapon. With a mocking smile on his face, he booted Red to one side to get a better view and flank the men who seemed to be confronting the woman. Knowing the move would mask the action, he slipped the loops off his pistols.

The rain had become a light drizzle, allowing him to see her when she spoke to him. She barely glanced his way. "It would have been easier to come up the trail."

"Lady," he said with a chuckle, "if I could have found the trail, I'd have used it. Are you Mrs. Davis?"

Looking surprised, the woman moved back a step so she could keep all of them in sight. "I'm Jessica Davis, but as you can see, I seem to have a situation here. I'm afraid I can't deal with any more guests right now."

He smiled at her attempt at humor, even if she sounded stressed and nervous. He decided she was one gutsy woman. "Mrs. Davis, I know that weapon is getting heavy, and please rest assured these gentlemen"—he stressed gentlemen for their benefit —"won't be bothering you anymore. You can go ahead and put the gun down. And ma'am? I know how strong the springs are on the hammers of that Greener, so you be real careful lettin' them down. That scattergun will take saints and sinners alike."

When she looked at him, there was relief and some small amount of amusement on her face. She pointed the Greener at the floor of the porch and carefully eased the hammers down one at a time. "Glad you happened to drop by."

He shook his head, keeping a watchful eye on the men. "Oh, I didn't just happen by. I've come to see you."

"Mister." The burly man on the ground finally decided he could put his foot down. "You got no call to horn in on this. And if you're calling on the woman, you can just take it somewhere else. She's already spoke for...by me. What's going on here is none of your business."

She interrupted before he could reply. "This man's name is Ezra King." She cut a glance toward

Coble. "Mr. King, I am neither spoken for nor willing to be entertained by you. That's my final word. Please leave."

The three other men aligned themselves toward Coble, stopping in a line like they were on a parade ground. They were dressed alike in black raincoats, low-pulled hats, glittering eyes, and a curious lack of anger. He didn't like them immediately because they'd had the foresight to dress for the rain. And it was a damned wet day.

He looked them over for a moment, hoping they wouldn't see him shiver with the cold. When no one spoke, he decided to force the issue.

"It'll come in handy, you boys wearing black."

Ezra took a step toward him, and his face led the advance with an unshaven jaw and forehead flat as a plate. "What's that supposed to mean?"

He didn't want this, but there are people you just can't talk to or out of their position. "I reckon you'll be dressed right for the burying. It would help to know if you're Methodist or Baptist...or whatever, so I know who to contact." In the strained silence that followed, along with the hissing of the rain, a red squirrel barked its irritation in the distance, and closer in...a wren fussed in the low-lying bushes. He calmly watched the men turning his comment over in their minds. His heart trip hammered as he watched Ezra's face pass through several shades of red.

Under the dripping porch, the woman crossed her arms and leaned against the rock wall of her home, studying him. Oddly enough, a slow smile turned the corner of her mouth and he was sure she gave a short nod, as if affirming something in her mind.

With arms crossed under her breasts and standing hipshot against the wall, he had to mentally shake himself to keep from being distracted by the sight she presented. It wasn't easy.

He half-looped the reins around the pommel with his left hand, his right resting on his hip, close to his gun. It was their move. "All right. I've bought chips in your game and called the bet. You need to call, or get the hell out of here."

Not taking his gaze from them, and glad they were still bunched up, he slowly hooked his thumb on the edge of his leather vest and moved it aside for them to see the star on his shirt.

"Just so there are no misunderstandings. Now, would you mind telling me why you're bothering this lady?"

Another shower of rain marched a drum on his hat, sluicing a cold stream down his back collar. Red grew restless, and Coble settled him with a gentle boot to the side.

A quiet voice came from one of the mounted men he'd already pegged as the leader in this bunch, just by the way he held himself.

"This is none of your damn business."

Coble speared the man with a hard gaze. "Mister, the minute you forced this lady to grab a shotgun, it became my business. I doubt I can see my way clear to stay out of it. Besides, I'm wet and cold. I'm tired, and my backside's sore as a boil. You'd better have a damned good reason for this."

When no answer came, he sighed noisily through a mouth gone dry. He really didn't want to draw a slippery-handled gun. "Well then, you boys better hightail it out of here. I don't know what your play is, but it's over."

"Like hell!" Ezra swept back his coat.

At any other time or place, the man would have looked ludicrous sporting all the guns he wore, but Coble knew these hills and the men who lived here —men who'd ridden the outlaw trail, men who carried five or six pistols with them because there wasn't time to reload in a fight.

Ezra faced him with two pistols set low in holsters and another in his belt for a cross-draw. He was a regular walking arsenal, but the man had lost his edge. He should have drawn first before he said anything. Coble calmly looked at him and waited, letting the tension draw out.

The quiet voice from the trio on his left spoke again, but he didn't move his attention from the man on the ground.

"Let it go, Ezra."

Ezra shook his head and ignored the advice. "Can't."

"I said let it go." With a note of exasperation at Ezra's lack of cooperation, the voice continued. "Then you better sharpen your teeth, Ezra. I got a feeling this marshal is going to be hard to chew."

"Not likely, he's not. That badge don't mean nothin' out here, and I don't like anybody buttin' in on our business." Ezra shifted his stance a little wider, grinning. "Matter of fact, you could've stole that badge. I don't know if you're the law at all."

"I'm the law," Coble said. "In these hills, or any other. You just back up. There's no need for a killing."

Ezra shook his head. "We're done talkin'."

"I said there's no need. Now back up."

The visibility wasn't good with the fog and rain, but he was close enough to see Ezra's eyes widen just before he grabbed the gun in his waistband.

When Ezra's hand touched the butt of his pistol, Coble shot him. With the rain-deadened sound ringing in his ears, he twisted around in the saddle, squinting through the powder smoke to confront the other three men, expecting a hail of bullets...and found nothing but churned earth and dripping foliage where the men disappeared into the forest. All but one.

Their leader sat waiting calmly, with his hands on the pommel of his saddle and rifle in its boot. His horse hadn't so much as twitched.

Coble watched the man a moment before he spoke. "Do you have a name, mister?"

The man debated the question a moment and then relented with a nod. "Billy Stiles."

He watched him closely, but Stiles seemed calm for just witnessing a shooting—nearly as calm as his horse. "I remember a Bill Stiles that used to live in these parts."

The man shook his head. "No relation."

Deciding the man offered no threat now, he holstered his gun. He hadn't touched the gun at his side, and Ezra hadn't seen the gun that killed him until too late.

"That's a cute trick, Marshal. Long gun on your hip and that short gun in a belly holster. I'll have to remember that."

"I'm pleased you like it," Coble said sarcastically. "Where'd your friends go?" Stiles smiled, and it wasn't a good smile. "They're around."

"So, what will it be? This going to end here, or do you want to pick up where Ezra left off?"

The question brought a long stare. "Ezra always thought he was a real stem-winder with a gun."

Shrugging, Coble eased himself in the saddle. "Just average. The thinking did him in. He should have done more thinking about plowing, or maybe blacksmithing. He had the hands for it."

He still couldn't see the other man very well. Stiles had his hat pulled down low and his face was in shadow. The rain came down harder again, rolling off his hat brim as lightning flashed and thunder rocked the hills around them.

Finally, Stiles spoke over the storm. "It's a bad time to be riding these hills, Marshal. A dangerous time."

Coble was curious about the man's attitude, and

it was a strange time for friendly conversation—and too damned wet. "My decision and law business."

"I assume you're going to Big Spring? Hell, everyone else is. You'll cause nothing but trouble."

"Any particular reason you don't want me around here?"

Stiles stood in his stirrups and stretched his back, hands still on the pommel, looking around the clearing. "These hills have a lot of history and not much of it good. Nobody trusts the law. The federals fight the ex-guerrillas. Blue-coat judges take all the land and sell it back to the rightful owners... for a profit, of course. Men have to steal to get the money to buy back their land and feed their families. Folks like that just get a mite skittish when a government man starts nosing around."

Coble knew the problem and the history along the border. Both sides were right, and wrong. There was no easy solution except complete and abject surrender by the locals—and that wasn't about to happen.

"The Army is here, and Caleb McGill is sheriff. Don't they keep the peace?"

Stiles chuckled. "Oh, sure they do. At least they try, but those Army boys, they're fresh, young kids from back east, and couldn't find a fly in an outhouse, and Caleb...well, he ain't been around much."

Coble's voice was cynical with his reply. "So, what? You're helping out? Vigilante? Baldknobbers?"

Stiles pointedly ignored the comment, but it

soured his expression. "You just got to this country, or I guess you did, and somehow you think you know everything? Just so you know. This wasn't my play, and things aren't always the way they look on first impression. Ezra was already here when we came, and he's been here before. He wouldn't have harmed that woman. Why are you here, Marshal? Are you looking to make a name for yourself by bringing in the last of the James Gang? The Younger brothers?"

He shook his head. "My interest is in a murdered girl. Nothing else."

"That killing was a bad thing. We had no part of that—don't know anyone who would. That's a fact." Stiles dismounted and turned the dead man over onto his back. He looked at him a moment and then took a silver dollar from his pocket and placed it over the wounds in Ezra's chest. "Two? Not many men can shoot like that. Who are you?"

"Coble Bray. I'm a deputy United States marshal."

A gasp came from the porch. "You took your sweet time getting here."

"I'm sorry about that, ma'am." He kept a weather eye on the other man. "I came as soon as I could, and your directions were just a little on the sparse side."

Grunting with exertion, Stiles dragged Ezra over to his horse, leaving twin trails in the grass growing between the smooth limestone patches that littered the yard. He jerked the reins down to make the horse stand in place and flung the limp body over the saddle. Slightly out of breath, he turned to speak again.

"That was good shootin', Marshal. But it won't do you much good. There are lots around that are faster. Hell, I've done better myself. You won't last long around here. I'd recommend that you leave."

"I guess we all have to die sometime...it just wasn't my turn today." He gave Stiles a two-fingered salute as he watched him ride out. For a long time he sat on Red, listening to the sound of the storm reverberating off the mountains, watching the lone figure with his load disappear into the slanting rain and trees beyond the meadow. He was lost in thought about why a man would endure the pounding rain just to give him a warning when he heard the woman's voice.

"You like sitting in the rain?"

He glanced at her with a smile and nudged Red up to the hitching rail. "No, ma'am, I surely don't."

Chapter Seven

COBLE WALKED TO THE PORCH AND GENTLY TOOK the shotgun from the woman's white-knuckled hands. He hadn't noticed her grab it up again. Maybe she wasn't too confident in his abilities. Or maybe she was going to help if things went bad?

"That was a brave thing, standing up to those men. You're quite a woman, Mrs. Davis." Standing close to her, he noted she was about his height, and he was taller than most. With a quick glance, he decided quite a woman wouldn't do her justice.

She stared at him with a blank expression like she was lost in thought, shook herself, and spoke briskly. "You'd best come inside. Looks like you're soaked to the bone."

He looked inside with longing but shook his head. "It wouldn't be proper, Mrs. Davis. I'd better follow those boys on into town, just to make sure they get there and stay put."

She graced him with a small smile and direct

gaze. "I'll decide what's proper in my house, Mr. Bray. With the rain, it's cold and noisy out here and we do need to talk. I don't intend to stand out here to do it. So please, come with me."

Following her, he paused at the threshold of the door and looked around the room. Seeing nothing unusual, he continued into the house.

Her voice was mocking. "You seem a little skittish. Not housebroke yet?"

"I'll admit to needing a little refinement." He chuckled as he leaned the Greener just inside the door. "What was all the ruckus about, if you don't mind me asking?"

"Oh, about what you'd expect." Her smile was rueful. "I'm a woman, alone, and I own a ranch. The man you shot thought I needed a husband to help me run it and spend my money. When I turned that down, he decided I needed a lover. When I laughed at him, which I shouldn't have done, he decided I should be taught a lesson."

"Well, I'd say that was a mite presumptuous of him," he said with a small smile. "Although, to be honest, no man likes to be laughed at when he offers himself up that way. We men are weak in that regard, and risky on his part. A lawyer told me once you shouldn't ask anything you don't already know the answer to—that advice was for people on the stand...and women."

He continued after a moment, afraid he'd overstepped propriety with his advice. "If you'd allow me, I do have one more suggestion."

She looked guardedly at him. "What is it?"

"The next time you point that shotgun at someone, especially under those circumstances, pull the trigger. There's no other reason to pick it up." He spoke again as she tried to interrupt. "No other reason, ma'am. You are a woman, alone, and I assume he was warned. You pull that trigger."

"Some don't find killing so easily done, Mr. Bray. That seems a bit bloodthirsty to me. I didn't see any need for killing him. I just wanted him to leave."

He was stung a little by the remark. But it wasn't the first time he'd been called bloodthirsty. Maybe he *was* too quick to shoot?

"You'd have found a reason soon enough, had I not ridden up to your door. And by then, your skirts may have been flying up over your head. You think about that before you hesitate again."

He glanced down at his feet, where the water dripping from his clothes darkened the braided rug.

She caught his glance. "You need to get out of those wet clothes before you catch a chill."

He considered that a moment while her right eyebrow slowly rose in an arch. Finally, deciding that arguing with this woman was fruitless, he conceded. "I'll just get my bedroll off old Red. I have some extras wrapped in an oilskin."

Outside, he took a moment to loosen the girth on the saddle as he took off the bedroll and saddlebags, and used the opportunity to look around. He was reasonably sure the local welcoming committee hadn't come back, but given the rain and dense brush and trees, a whole herd of Comanche could have been hiding a few steps away and he'd never know it. Dodging a friendly nip from Red, he turned and headed back into the house.

"Is there a place I can change?" He was already shivering, so by the time she pointed toward a room to his right, he'd shucked his guns and hung the belt on a peg by the door. "I'll just be a moment. Do I smell coffee?"

"Of course." She stared at the worn walnut grips on his pistols nestled in their holsters. "I always have a pot on."

Seeing her staring at his gun belt, he spoke softly. "He really didn't give me much choice, Mrs. Davis."

Startled, she gave a little jump and then looked at him. "I understand that...at least, I think I do. In theory. It's just...I remembered something Caleb said, back when we were talking about you."

The silence stretched out. In a way, he was curious, but not too much. "And?"

He kept his eyes on the rawhide strings holding his blanket roll together, hands busy doing nothing.

She took a deep breath. "Caleb said trouble hangs over you like a cloud, and people die when you come around. He even made some mention of the pale rider in the book of Revelation. Once I heard your name, I felt sorry for Ezra, because I knew what was coming. He never had a chance."

"And knowing all that, not believing in killing, you still sent for me." He looked at her for a moment and then nodded slowly. "Caleb's a good man." He shrugged. "Talks a bit too much, but still...rarely wrong. And Ezra had his chance."

They stared at each other for a few moments past proper, then he turned toward the bedroom. Closing the door, he spread the blanket roll on the bed. Shaking out the oilskin, he put it on the floor and quickly undressed, dropping his wet clothes on the skin. After he dried himself with a piece of old rag and dressed in dry clothes, he rolled the wet ones up in the skin and tied the bundle together.

Feeling warmer now that he was dry, he looked around the room. It was a history lesson waiting to be learned. The furniture in the room, what there was of it, was sturdy and handmade. The skill of the carpenter was apparent by the smoothness of the oak bed posts, and a deep red wardrobe appeared to be made from cherry wood. Where had the builder gotten the wood? Not many cherry trees in this part of the country, at least not big enough for planks. The one window in the room had glass panes, which must have been hauled in with no small amount of trouble, and the shutters were on the inside, to be closed in case of attack or in the dead of winter.

Another lesson was the bed with one pillow, with a worn comforter. The wardrobe door was ajar and held a scant amount of clothes and one pair of good shoes for Sunday meeting. This woman had seen good times, but life had dealt her an unfair hand. How would finding her daughter's killer change that?

The room had a reading table next to the bed, in front of the window, to take advantage of the light. A large Bible was opened to the center where all the weddings and deaths were recorded.

Her daughter's death had been entered six weeks ago. Elaine Davis, aged 12. Murdered. There was what looked like a water spot on the page, and he imagined a tear falling and a smudge as she tried to wipe it away. Her husband had been dead over a year, and their marriage had lasted twelve. Unfair hands were sometimes dealt in pairs. This woman had endured a lot, and frontier women must surely suffer more than most.

He ran his hand over the Bible with movements not unlike a caress and noticed a lace bookmark at the text of Deuteronomy nineteen, where the twenty-first verse spoke of revenge and of an eye for an eye. Remembering the anger in her letter to him, he turned the pages to the book of John and placed the marker there to offer her some hope and comfort. He expected she'd taught her daughter well, and that should help her grief and anger.

———

HER BACK WAS TURNED when he came out of the bedroom, so he took a moment to look the place over. There were only three rooms and a pantry to the house. She was in the kitchen, with the great room holding a well-fitted limestone fireplace. There was a loft above where the daughter had likely slept. It would be the warmest place in the winter but unbearable in the summer. The pantry had a door in it, and it probably opened to a smoke-house or shed sometimes used for cooking.

She picked up two pewter cups filled with coffee and walked toward him. "Sit at the table, Mr. Bray. I can have a bit of lunch ready in a few minutes if you like."

Seated at the table facing each other, they were intimately close, yet she didn't shy away. No false modesty here, and he liked that about her. He chided himself with that thought. Ever since he'd first laid eyes on her, he'd been finding things he liked about her. It was time to get to business before he became too distracted.

He rose and went to the coat tree where his gun belt hung, retrieved the two revolvers, pulled a blue bandanna from his back pocket, and sat again. He began drying the pistols, dropping the ramrods down to pull the pins that held in the cylinders, and working on each. With his hands busy, drying each part carefully, he looked at her.

"So. Tell me a story. How does a young girl disappear around here and be found a week later, murdered?"

She visibly gathered herself before she answered. "I wish there were more to tell. Elaine, my daughter, rode into town for supplies. It's only a mile or so. As best we can tell, she never made it to town. And she never came back." She stopped a moment and continued in a choked voice. "At least, not alive."

"Was that something she did often? Ride alone?"

She nodded. "Elaine loved to ride. It's not far to town. I never thought..."

"Nobody would. Not in a settled community like this." Trying to sidetrack her guilt, he prodded for more information. "Who found her?"

It took her a moment to answer. "The Army. Captain Meyers, I believe. And then Caleb brought her home to me."

He nodded, eyes on his job. "Where was she found?"

"I'll have to show you. It wouldn't do any good to tell you unless you're familiar with the country."

"So, it was out in the woods, somewhere?"

She nodded. "It was, but pretty close to a well-used trail."

He thought a moment and came up with a question that had been bothering him and was hard to ask. "Did a doctor or Army surgeon look at her after she was brought in?"

She seemed startled and stared at him a moment. "I don't think so. They took her into town, and Caleb brought her to me right away. I was grateful for that. She wouldn't want anyone to see her that way. Why does it matter?"

He glanced up. "Just wondered how long she'd been dead when they found her."

She gave him a funny look. "What difference would it...you mean..." She paused as the inference of what he was really wondering became clear to her. How long was she captive? How long was she used?

"But she was only twelve. Oh, god."

"I'm sorry to upset you, but it's a question that has to be asked."

"I still don't see why. How can that help my daughter?"

This wasn't the usual thing he dealt with, and he didn't know the best way to proceed. Finally, he decided on the truth. "Nothing will help your daughter. Your daughter's gone. We can't do anything about that. But if I'm to find her killer, I need to understand him. A man's not much different than any other animal. Once you understand his nature, then you have a good chance of predicting his path. For now, I can only understand the killer by what he's done or not done. An old medicine man of the Otoe told me once that he would shadow my trail, smell the smoke from my fire, eat my food, and listen to my dreams at night...and after that, he would control me and kill me at his leisure because he would know my soul."

Her eyes widened, not sure whether to believe him. "You must have really made him mad. Has he followed you?"

"I don't know. He stole a horse from me. I stole him back along with a couple of others, and he was mad enough to call down lightning. Maybe he's out there, sneaking around. Sometimes, when the wind's blowing at night, I imagine I can hear him. He was a wise man, that Indian." He laughed. "Not much of a horse thief, though." He began re-assembling the revolvers. "What about your husband?"

"What?" She was so startled by the conversation's change of direction she nearly dropped her cup.

He was watching her, and she brought up a yearning in him. She was a pretty woman. "Your husband. How did he die?"

She sighed and put her coffee cup on the table, took up a towel made from a feed sack, and wiped a drop of coffee off the table. Looking flustered, she tried to put back an errant lock of hair.

"You're avoiding the question, Mrs. Davis. Is it that hard?"

She gave a little shrug and tossed the towel on the table. "No, it's not a difficult question. I just wasn't expecting it." She sighed again, loneliness and frustration evident on her face. "My husband was coming home after dark a little over a year ago. His horse stepped off the trail, it was steep there. The horse rolled on him. The saddle horn crushed his chest. We didn't find him until morning." She shook her head. "That jug-headed horse. He wasn't a good night-horse, and we both knew it. But my husband dearly liked him."

He nodded. it was a story that happened all too often. Sometimes people just disappeared and were never found from just such an accident. "A tough way to go. He was a fine mason and carpenter."

Her gaze met his. "How do you...?"

"It's easy if you look around. This house was

made by a man good with his hands, a man who appreciated wood and stone and took the time to do something right." He paused a moment and looked directly at her. "He was also excellent in his choice of women."

She gave him a frank smile and he liked the twinkle in her eyes. "What makes you think he chose me and not the other way around?"

He stared at her a little too long, lost for a moment in those steady blue eyes contrasting so starkly with her dark hair.

"Do I get to ask you a question, Mr. Bray?"

"Maybe we should quit being so formal."

"Now who's dodging?"

Holding the longer-barreled Remington, he quarter-cocked the hammer and spun the cylinder, then let the hammer down on an empty chamber. He nodded at her. "Go ahead."

"The man you just killed. Does that bother you?" She shuddered and crossed her arms across her chest. "It just seemed so sudden and senseless."

"Well, conversation kind of dried up. And it wasn't sudden. It may not have seemed like it, but he had a choice and made his decision with people telling him not to. And to answer your question, no, it doesn't bother me." Then, thinking of the sleepless nights and his friend Priest, he relented and nodded his head. "Well, sometimes it does. That's to be expected, I guess."

She shook her head again, her expressive eyes looking past him at something only she could see.

"Why did you kill him? Couldn't you have just shot him in the arm or something?"

He chuckled, looked at her, and then laughed outright. "That works good in those stories you see printed in the paper or those dime novels that are showing up from back east. Unfortunately, the real thing is never what people imagine it to be. Maybe I'm not that good of a shot. The man was trying to kill me. It wasn't target practice with lots of time to aim."

"And the others? I understand that, in your line of work, you have killed many men. What about them?"

"Mrs. Davis..."

She arched an eyebrow at him.

"I believe we can stop being so formal, don't you? Please, call me Jessica."

"Why all the questions? I've heard less when someone was buying a horse. I feel like you're checking my teeth and making sure I'm not swaybacked."

"Already done that," she said seriously. "And yes, I'm trying to pull an Otoe on you."

He thought a moment, feeling this was an important juncture between them, even though they'd just met.

"All right. Yes. It bothers me, if I let it. Most folks have a lifetime of hurt and worries. You learn to deal with it, to put it away. I've always believed the mind is a room with many doors. Most of the doors you pass through all the time. Some of them you open on occasion to see what's in there and reminisce. A few of the doors...well, you kind of tiptoe by them so you won't wake up what is inside. Then there are those special doors you nail shut and you never open them. Not ever."

He stood abruptly, the legs of the chair scraping the floor beneath him. "And with that deep thought, I'd better get going. The rain has stopped and I want to get to Big Springs before dark."

When he tried to pick up his bundle of wet clothing, she stopped him. "Just leave those here. I'll hang them out to dry when the sun comes out."

"All right."

She stood close to him, close enough to smell or even taste if he wanted to, and he noticed her dark hair had red in it that changed in the light. He took a deep breath.

"Again, I'm sorry for your troubles and sorry I couldn't get here sooner. We'll work our way through this."

She smiled at him. "Thank you. I guess I just have some doors to close and find the right locks for them."

"Nails, Jessica. Use nails. Locks can be picked."

Chapter Eight

COBLE WASN'T FAR DOWN THE TRAIL WHEN HE realized he didn't get that lunch she'd promised. The rain had stopped and the sun was trying to peek out. He stopped Red in a small glade amid tendrils of fog and mist from the rapidly rising temperature, pulled a bag of pemmican from his saddlebag, and paused to think a mite.

Most people thought he just confronted the bad guys and challenged them to shoot it out, or walked in with guns blazing and the devil take the hindmost.

Nothing could be farther from the truth.

One of the things that made him effective was his desire to know just what he was getting into. He liked to know about his opponent, and just as much about the supporting players. If you separate the bull from the herd, sometimes they're not as dangerous. If you confront a lone gunman at a saloon or on the street, like as not, he won't be baited into a fight. There's too much to lose with not much gain.

However, if you confront the same person when he's surrounded by people, he can't lose face and will accept the challenge. So Coble liked to know all the different things affecting a situation before taking action. Usually. Sometimes fate took a hand in that.

What did he know that hadn't been in the letter? Not much. The men who were threatening Jessica probably had nothing to do with her troubles. They just saw an opportunity and tried to take it. It was their tough luck they'd run into the resolve of a good woman.

After his slow approach into this country, it was no surprise to him someone could snatch the girl unobserved, or anyone for that matter. That part would be easy. This was ambush country, no doubt about it. What did he need to pursue now?

After a few weeks passing, he didn't put much stock in finding a trail. But wild as these hills were, it was a pretty close-knit community. Everyone would know, or at least know of, all their neighbors who lived around here. The kidnapping of the girl along a dense trail would be a simple matter, but to keep someone captive a week with no one else seeing anything, now that would be a trick.

And where would someone keep a captive? A cabin? Cave? Someone's house in town? There were too many questions, and not enough answers.

He needed to talk to Caleb. He would know where to start. But first, a meal and a real bed.

The trail into Big Springs was canopied by oak and sycamore, the road green with a lush growth of grass that showed little travel, meandering around limestone outcroppings across the small creeks—running fuller now since the rain. The only tracks were from Stiles and the rest of the boys that had gone before him. He didn't realize how much time he'd spent with Jessica until he saw the long shadows from the sun, signaling the day was nearly over.

He pushed Red on toward Big Springs.

After the rain stopped and the storm marshaled its ships together and pushed them away to the east, the tops of the clouds caught sunlight, a picture showing sails of gold and white. In the gathering dusk, the hills surrounding Big Springs held myriad shades of green and brown as the setting sun gave up its light. Hues of purple and black crept closer to the town along the base of the hills, leaving the peaks a brilliant green in the fading light. Beautiful country...hiding death.

———

ALFRED *POP* JANUS perched precariously on the rear legs of his cane-backed chair, barely leaning against the wall of Ziler's Mercantile and Hardware. He enjoyed the coolness sweeping down the street and the clean smell after the rain, savoring the quietness of the evening with the sureness of someone who'd traveled a lot of miles in his day...and his day was a long time ago.

His sharp eyes, not dimmed by the passage of years, picked out movement at the end of the street. Curious, he leaned forward for a better look, aware the shadows would hide him from casual view.

A lone man materialized at the end of the street, riding slowly toward him. The slow rhythm of the horse's hooves preceded them up the street. He slouched in the saddle like a plainsman and seemed to be looking the place over.

Two minutes passed and the man drew even with him. Sheriff Stiles had ridden in earlier with a body draped over a saddle.

Then this man rode in. Coincidence?

The man straightened in the saddle, took off the limp hat with his left hand, and beat it against the pommel of his saddle, his right never straying far from the gun on his hip.

Recognition came like a bolt of lightning. Coble Bray.

Pop herded cattle from Texas to Colorado and had seen boomtowns die and bloody Indian wars all over the country. History had chiseled the lines on his face, and time the rheumatism in his withered back. He was old, but he knew a warrior when he saw one. He'd seen this one before, and heard a lot about him since.

Where men sat around lonely campfires or nursed a beer bought with their last two bits, the talk would be of wild horses and cattle stampedes, and of good women and bad. Then the talk would be of guns and the men who used them just a little better than their peers, and of the outlaws who couldn't be brought in, like bad mustangs that couldn't be tamed...and more often than not, the talk would turn to Coble Bray.

Lessons come hard for some men, and he was the last page in their study book. Big Jim McSweeney in Dodge City. Saber Collins in Springfield, who'd previously killed four lawmen who tried to take him in. The McCandless boys over in the nation. Three of them had braced the marshal in the Indian Agent's sutlery. And died. He'd taken lead in that one, but walked away under his own power.

A lone gun, even during the war, rumored to work behind enemy lines.

Disappeared after the war, reported to be in another country...in another war. Again, rumored. Then, he showed up working for a carpetbagger judge. And again, a lone gun. Sent to serve warrants to men living on the fringe of society, the men so mean and dirty, or so very, very good, that no ordinary lawman could bring them in. When the cost in lawmen seemed too high, they sent for Coble Bray.

What Pop couldn't figure out? Why was he here in Big Springs, and who was going to die because of it?

COBLE LOOKED at the old man straddling the chair on the porch and spoke to him. "Evening, old timer." His voice seemed to jolt the man from his thoughts.

The chair abruptly came down on all four legs with a bang.

"It is that." The old man seemed surprised he'd stopped by to talk.

He studied the codger a moment. Something about him tickled his memory. "Can you point me to the sheriff's office?"

"Reckon so. Office is right on down the street. Left side, by the bank. Cain't miss it." The old man chuckled. "Kind of convenient, don't you think? Bein' by the bank?"

He got the inference, remembering his warning to Frank in Kansas City. "Depends on who comes calling."

"You're calling."

"Not my line of work."

The old man harumphed. "Well, it don't matter. Them days are gone, friend. With Jesse runnin' off, that sort of thing's the least of our worries. The boys are mostly scattered and ain't dumb enough to mess in their own nest."

He nodded, suddenly tired to the bone. "I'd have to agree with that one, old timer."

The codger peered closer at him. "Had trouble?"

Coble sighed. "Some." He paused. "More'n I need."

The old man suddenly became cagey. "Maybe you'd better tread light until you read the sign around here. You're in Injun country. There's a bad crowd in these parts."

"I've seen a few bad crowds."

The old timer chuckled. "Yeah, I reckon you have."

His memory finally kicked in and he peered closer under the awning. "That laugh sounds familiar. Do I know you?"

"Not really, but I've been around some of the places you were. And I'm a friend of Caleb's. I'm Pop Janus."

Coble pulled the name up from memories of a cattle drive and later some shooting trouble in Abilene. "I've heard the name, and if you're a friend of Caleb's, that's good enough for me. It's always nice to have a friend around." He sat straight in the saddle, stretching his back. "I'd best be checkin' in with McGill."

"If you are expecting to see McGill at the sheriff's office, you're wasting your time."

"Why?" He turned back toward Pop with a puzzled frown. "Is he gone somewhere?"

"He's gone, all right. Gone as in fired. The town council fired him a few days ago."

He thought a moment, slowly shaking his head. "Who's the new sheriff?"

"Billy Stiles. Good man, but full of himself. Them kind's always dangerous."

Coble looked sharply at Pop. "I met him earlier today. Is he kin to Bill Stiles? Rode with Bloody Bill and them a long time ago?"

"Nope. But he might as well be. He's young but handy, and seems to have a lot of deputies, if you know what I mean."

He thought about that one a moment. "Anyone else around I should know about?"

"Just one I can think of that you'd need to worry about. You ever hear of Onofrio Perez?" He pronounced the last name *Pear-rez*. "He's been hangin' around. And there's some men call themselves Baldknobbers. They're mostly drygulchers that try to keep their names secret, but it ain't very hard to nose them out. They've been ridin' the vigilante trail, and ain't too particular about who gets strung up, if you know what I mean. This country's headed for grief. People are afraid, and there's a lot of folk ridin' scared."

Coble thought about that a moment. There wasn't anything more dangerous than a bunch of scared citizenry.

"Thanks, Pop. And be careful of that chair. Way you're riding it, you'll likely get throwed."

Pop gave an indignant snort. "Hell, you're wrong there, son. She tried it once, but I rode her all the way down. Never mussed a hair on my head."

Coble lightly gigged his horse to get him

moving. "If I remember right, you don't have much hair."

As he rode off, Pop called to his retreating back. "Things get tight, I'll be around." Then, in a voice so quiet he could barely hear, he said, "And where you are, things always get tight."

He rode down the street, cataloging the storefronts and side alleys the best he could in the fading light, getting a picture in his mind of the town's layout. You never know when you might need that kind of information in a hurry.

Big Springs had been born of necessity next to a huge spring of cold, clear water that never dried up and pushed millions of gallons into the nearby White River. Nestled at the bottom of a valley, the town looked like a child had glued the buildings to the bottom of a coffee cup.

The main street ran along the bottom of the valley, the only flat place in town. All the stores were along the street, with the rest of the homes and buildings on the surrounding hills. Some perched precariously with stilts holding up the fronts and their backs buried into the mountain. One exception was a church, sitting on a small knoll overlooking the town. The white-painted walls were bright against the darkening background of the hills. A path, bordered with white rocks, wound its way up to the sanctuary. A small house matched the church in color, and both buildings framed a cemetery in the back. He idly wondered how they dug through the rocks that must be there to do the burying.

The buildings on both sides of the street resembled most towns he'd been in—just the names were painted in different places. The sign at the local café read Restaurant and Lunchroom. As he rode by, he saw tables covered with red-checked tablecloths and most were full of evening patrons.

A man stopped to glance at him as he locked up his store and then scurried around the corner between buildings. The sign on his store read Workman's, but the light was poor and he couldn't tell what kind of merchandise the store sold.

There were people on both sides of the street, some walking determinedly toward unknown destinations, others stopping to stare at him as he rode by. Few women were seen on the street, but he didn't see that as odd. It was suppertime, the world over.

Like most lawmen, he took interest in the saloon right away. The Gold Emporium would easily be the largest building in town, taking up at least three spaces that businesses had once occupied. Its center façade rose higher than the adjoining buildings.

He had a purely professional interest. The saloon was generally the main source of trouble in any town, but always the best clearinghouse of information. Men often used such places for business meetings and queries about things for sale, like cattle, or just for blowing off steam. There were no side doors to the place, meaning if there was a back door to the place, it actually was in the back. He filed the information away for future reference and shuffled his horse on toward the sheriff's office.

Next to the Big Springs Bank, a small building sported a sign labeled Sheriff. He headed his horse into the hitch rail. The building appeared narrow on the front, with bars on the windows, but went a long way back. He'd always wondered if the bars kept prisoners in or people out. The boardwalk sported an awning held up by four pillars that didn't look like they could take the weight of the rain that had fallen that day.

The benches in front of the office were full of rough-looking men lounging haphazardly enough to block entry to the door. Two of the hard-eyed men wore long black coats, and he thought of Pop's comment about the sheriff having too many deputies.

All eyes were on him as he dismounted, keeping the horse between him and the men. He shucked his Henry rifle when he stepped down, resting it across the saddle and pointing at the jail. Hidden from the eyes of the men on the porch, he slipped the thong from the hammer of his pistol.

"I'm looking for the sheriff."

One of the men hawked and spat a stream of tobacco juice onto the boardwalk. "What do you want him for?"

"None of your damned business."

While the man tried to think of a reply that

wouldn't get him shot, the door to the jail opened. A voice shouted from inside, "Come on in."

He hesitated. "Better if you come outside, Sheriff Stiles."

A young man with curly brown hair stuck his head out the door and grinned at him. He was medium-sized with wide shoulders, quick blue eyes set in a squarish head, and seemed to be all muscle from the neck down. Starting to walk on out, he stopped.

"Murphy, get your damned feet out of the door."

The man in question fairly leaped to obey while the others sat up straight. Murphy seemed to have less trouble deciphering the sheriff's orders than Coble's comments.

At first glance, the sheriff seemed young for the job, but the man had a steady look to him Coble recognized. He looked young, but this man had handled his share of trouble. And they'd met earlier in the day.

Stiles stood on the boardwalk with his hands on his hips. "So, you going to shoot me, or do we talk?"

Coble regarded the man a moment and then slid the Henry back into the rifle's boot. Coming around the front of Red, he looped the reins over the rail and stepped up on the walk.

He pointed back inside the jail. "You're some drier than the last time we met. Let's have that talk."

Stiles turned and walked back inside and he followed. The sheriff went straight to a cluttered desk taking up one corner. A single door led to the jail in the back. Other than a cast-iron stove in the center of the room and a gun rack, the only other furniture in the room consisted of a few chairs against the far wall and a single cot with rumpled blankets.

He pulled a chair over to sit opposite the sheriff, turned it around, and leaned on the back as he sat. "I usually check in with the local sheriff when I come to a town. Since we've already met, I don't have to extend that courtesy."

Stiles inclined his head a fraction. "Noted and appreciated. Anything else? Have a nice visit with the widow?"

Coble looked at him. A strange comment to someone who'd just rode in. "Like I've said, my interest is in the Davis girl. You got any ideas on who killed her?"

Stiles leaned over and pulled open a drawer of the desk. He reached inside and tossed a hank of black hair on the desktop. "We found this scalp on an Indian a few days ago."

Coble picked up the hard, withered scalp and fingered it a moment, then tossed it back down. "What's going on here, Stiles? That scalp might have come from your grandmother, but not a young girl."

The man's gaze was mocking. "Not your problem, Marshal, so you can trot on back to Kansas or wherever you came from."

They stared at each other a long moment and

then Stiles continued with a sigh. "Look, the town wanted closure. Things were getting out of hand. The judge is in town and is going to make a run for the governorship soon and he wants closure on this little problem in a big hurry." He held up the scalp. "We have closure."

"What about the Indian you found it on?"

Stiles shrugged. "He died."

"Handy."

Stiles grinned at him. "Can't deny that."

Coble stood abruptly, causing the sheriff to flinch. "That dog won't hunt, Sheriff. A child could figure out something is wrong here."

The sheriff smiled at him, shaking his head and leaning back in his chair. "Oh, that dog will hunt. It's been howling at the moon for a long while. And you'd best stay out of the woods, Marshal. I've got all the dogs, and all the hunters."

"I can't see myself doing that."

"Your funeral."

Coble turned as three men filed into the room, lining up across the door. No guns were drawn, but it wouldn't take much. Even a stubborn mule can recognize a stone wall when he sees it. He gave a small smile and nod to Stiles and started toward the door. He stopped in front of the three men who'd entered behind him, studying their faces. None met his eyes. They looked to Stiles for direction.

At what he supposed was a signal from the sheriff, the man in front of him stepped aside with a shrug of regret and a small smile on his face.

"Do I know you?" He could have moved on, but stood in front of the man.

"Nope. Not yet. Name's Johnny Cade. We haven't met."

He nodded. Just what he needed—another wannabe bad man. "Texas Johnny Cade. I've heard the name, but I haven't seen any paper put out on you. Not yet anyway. You got an honest job around here, or are you working for the sheriff?"

Cade didn't rise to the bait. "I'll look forward to seeing you again, Marshal. Real soon."

He shook his head in disgust, looking the young man in the eye. "Take my word for it, Johnny. No reputation's worth dying for."

Never being fond of verbal dueling, he paused at the hitch rail, his thoughts racing. The town council fired McGill, who worked here for years, and then hired a young sheriff. Stiles was hiring the very men he should be putting in jail. Curious, but not unheard of. It was a free country and people could do whatever they wanted—good or bad.

Still thinking it through, he swung up on Red. Stiles had said they wanted a quick resolution. Why? The governorship? Doubtful. That didn't ring true with the judge he remembered. But he could be wrong. Maybe investigating the murder of the girl was interfering with something else they had going on? Or maybe someone pulling the strings had something to do with the murder. He turned Red back down the street toward the Gold Emporium. His thoughts turned to something to eat and some sleep in a real bed. Then he'd hit the trail. Until he talked to McGill, what direction he'd go was a toss-up. He had about zero investigative skills, at least in a formal sense. His experience was simple, track someone down and bring them back to stand trial, or shoot it out. Sometimes it angered him that the people he was sent to bring in were the very ones that would not come back.

He guessed his skills needed to change.

Chapter Nine

"TIME TO GO."

The young girl struggled to raise her head, struggled to pull herself from the abyss of her nightmares that were reality.

Reality was a collage of painful memories, dreamlike and clouded, as hunger and thirst weakened her to the point of collapse.

"Come." The voice, low and soothing, seemed disembodied, belonging to a face leaning toward her out of the mist.

Finally, she stirred. "Please, mister. Let me go. I won't tell anyone. Please?"

"You will be free this day," the soothing voice said.

Hope burst forth in her eyes, then clouded at his next words. "Do you want to be saved, child? You must be saved to go free."

"Yes," she finally said, instinctively knowing the price. "I want to be saved." It seemed they had walked for hours, and at the end, she finally collapsed and had to be carried. Like coming out of a deep sleep, she struggled to sit up.

Looking down at herself, she saw pine needles clinging to her naked body and feebly attempted to brush at them with hands she couldn't feel.

"Stand up." The voice came from behind her.

She raised her head and saw a crude wooden cross in front of her that looked woven with grapevines and twigs. As she stood, her knees trembled and shook. Her arms hung limply at her sides. Her mind tried to will her body to move, to run, but her legs barely quivered at the thought.

Turning her head, she tried to speak and, failing that, turned her face away from the man behind her. A dry sob racked her thin chest. She wanted to cry but hadn't had a drink of water in two days. Tears just wouldn't come.

"Be still." Hands came from behind her, moving over her body with a caressing touch, cleaning all the dirt and needles from her skin.

"Kneel, child. Kneel before the cross."

Weakly, she dropped to her knees, the earth digging into her flesh. "Lean forward, child. Touch your forehead to the ground in supplication. Pray for your soul."

"No more. Please."

"What is your name, child? Speak your name so it will be written in the Book of Life."

"Isabel. Isabel Jakes."

At the end, she didn't feel fear. What she felt

was nothing at all. When the cold steel caressed her throat, she didn't flinch but smiled as her head was pulled back by her hair. She welcomed the knife. She welcomed release.

———

FULL DARKNESS HAD FALLEN while Coble was inside the sheriff's office, and the street was dark and brooding. Or maybe it was just his mood. A pool of light fronted the stable barn, provided by oil lanterns hanging on the doors. In the other direction, Gold's Emporium was open, along with the Commercial Hotel. Since neither place was likely to close, he walked his horse down to the stable.

The double doors to the barn were open, but no one was around. It was dark inside so he took one of the lanterns hanging on the door. Amid fragrant smells common to stables the world over, he stripped the saddle from his horse and settled him in an empty stall, helping himself to a bucket of water and some oats for Red's feedbag.

"You'll probably eat better than me tonight." His voice was soft as he scratched the horse behind the ears. Red snorted in his oats and tried to step on his foot, but it wasn't a really serious effort. The horse was content. After rubbing him down with an old burlap sack and taking off the feedbag, he closed the stall door, slung his saddlebags and blanket roll over his shoulder, and grabbed his rifle.

He walked up the boardwalk, his heels softly

scuffing on the planks, pausing at the door to the Emporium. Through the door, the saloon looked cleaner than most, with a bar stretching the full width of the building. Behind the bar was a long mirror, and on each side were paintings of women with impossible proportions. There were some poor shots among the clientele, at least on some occasions. Someone had tried to use the nipples on one of the paintings for target practice. Now the woman in the painting had three. Strange. One side of the room held several poker tables and two pool tables, one with the smaller pockets of the newly popular snooker table.

The other side, the one closest to the stairs leading to the upper floor rooms, was cleared for a dance floor, with small tables ringed around it. It was early yet, but the room was mostly full. The bar girls and waitresses bustled between tables, both selling their particular wares.

Years of practice enabled him to scan the room quickly, looking for potential trouble just waiting to happen, but things looked tame. Hardly breaking stride, he continued past to the Commercial Hotel.

Inside, a door connected to the restaurant, and his grumbling belly caused him to make a hard right into the eatery. The room wasn't large, and most of the tables were taken. Looking around for a seat, he heard a familiar voice call his name.

Judge Johnstone sat at a long table with several people. The judge was a man with an overly large head and an immense amount of slicked-back hair, and he dressed in a dapper suit with a broadcloth vest.

He'd never cared for the man, but took the jobs he offered because of the office he held. Now, in a few short hours after learning of the firing of McGill and appointing Stiles, the man just looked like another slick lawyer to him.

Another thought crossed his mind, and he could almost hear the Priest talking. *Perception is reality. And perceptions change.*

The judge motioned him to an empty space across the table from him.

Making his way to the table, amid stares from the locals, he extended his hand across the table and greeted the man. He was still surprised the judge was here because he hardly ever left the confines of his chambers.

"It's been a while. You're a long way from Fort Smith."

"Have a seat, Marshal." The judge shook his hand, and the grip was strong. "You remember my adjutant, Lieutenant Evans?"

Evans nodded at him but didn't extend his hand. Not that he would expect it. Lieutenant Evans was a man who believed in law and order but didn't believe in killing or violence. Apparently everyone was just supposed to do what the lieutenant said. All the time, and every time. He held Evans's look a moment, smiled slightly, and then switched his attention to the officer on the judge's right.

This man extended his hand with a small smile,

not missing the byplay. "David Meyers, Marshal. Pleased to meet you."

"My pleasure, Captain. You've had a rough time of it." And he meant it, knowing this man had earned his bars in the field, not in an office like the adjutant. This was a line officer, a veteran of many battles, and in the one glance, he could feel the man's frustration, see it lying behind his eyes.

The man looked down but almost immediately returned his gaze to Coble. "If you are here to investigate the girl's killing, more power to you. I'd rather have done anything than find that girl."

"I'd like to talk to you later, if that's all right?"

The judge couldn't be held out of a conversation very long. "He'll be available, but I don't think it will be necessary. You've talked to the sheriff?"

Coble shook his head and stared at the judge. "Oh, I talked to him all right. I heard his stories and saw some of his dirty work. There's nothing about it that passes muster."

The judge sat up straight in his chair. "Now, don't go runnin' off half-cocked. It's a theory that'll put the matter at rest, and I'm satisfied with it. This part of the country could blow apart with all the bad feelings going around. This matter needs to be settled. Now."

Coble let his gaze cover the three men. The judge and Lt. Evans looked defiantly at him. Meyers studied the intricate designs on the tablecloth.

"How about you, Captain?" Coble asked. "I'm guessing you've seen a few scalps in your time."

When no one replied, he continued with a sigh. "Well, I will admit that I'm not much of a detective, and I just got to town, but I already know a couple of things for a fact. Sheriff Stiles is a liar and quite possibly a murderer."

He caught a smile from Captain Meyers before Evans exploded at him. "Dammit, man, how can you say that? Stiles is a duly appointed official."

"Duly appointed doesn't make him honest. I'd be careful not to be painted with the same brush." He ignored Lieutenant Evans then, speaking instead to the judge. "You mind if I look into it?"

Johnstone hesitated a moment, obviously trying to control his anger, his salt and pepper mutton-chops quivering a moment, and then spoke. "Yes, I do mind. It's over." He held up his hand, palm out, toward Coble. "I know what you're thinking, but even if the Indian didn't do it, we'll never find that girl's killer in this godforsaken brush country. It just took you too long to get here. The trail is cold. The matter has been handled. And, Marshal..."

The judge looked steadily at Coble. "You wouldn't want to do anything to jeopardize your position. You've not been invited here in any official capacity, so there is no stigma if you just turn around and leave. That's what I am asking you to do. You have a job, and you do it well. It just isn't here. And not now."

Coble shifted his gaze to Captain Meyers. Cool and detached, the captain gazed steadily back at him. He wouldn't want those eyes looking at him down the barrel of a rifle.

"Well then, I guess that takes care of that." He started away, then turned back. "One thing you're wrong about, Judge. I will find out who killed this girl, and they will be dealt with. As far as my not being here in any official capacity, this is in my territory. I do not need your invitation. Be careful that you don't jeopardize your own position. I've been requested by the local sheriff who was elected by the people of this county. My help has been requested by a long-standing and aggrieved citizen of this county. That's enough for me."

For the first time, he realized there was an audience when they were interrupted by people clapping their hands and a few gruff cheers.

The judge's face was close to the same color of red that showed in the checkered tablecloth. "Stiles is the local sheriff now, with my full authority, and he didn't request your help."

Coble calmly shrugged, perversely enjoying the encounter. It cleared the air on many things. "Stiles is a joke and a hired killer."

With both the judge and his adjutant yelling at him, he turned and walked away. His appetite displaced by anger, he returned to the hotel desk and signed for a room.

"Staying long"—the desk clerk turned the ledger and glanced at his name—"Mr. Bray?"

"Depends," Coble snapped.

"On what?" The clerk was always alert to any gossip floating around.

His temper was cooling already, so he started the cliché. "Circumstances."

"Which are altered by circumstances...I know." The thwarted clerk gave a weary sigh, then handed him a key. "Room number fourteen. Up the stairs and the last door on the left. Enjoy your stay."

Coble started away when a sudden thought occurred. "One thing. Is the judge and his party staying at the hotel?"

"Now, you know I can't..."

He slid a twenty-dollar gold piece across the counter but kept his hand on it. The clerk looked at the money, then up at him. "They've been here about two weeks."

He took his hand off the gold piece. "You know what they're doing here?"

"They don't say." The gold piece greased the wheels, and the clerk was eager to talk. "But it's pretty easy to figure. I think the judge is looking for a higher office, maybe governor? Every day or so, a different politician will show up to talk with them. I guess the judge figures this is an out-of-the-way place with no reporters around. And"—the man leaned closer with his secret—"he must be looking for a new wife because he's been trying out several applicants, if you know what I mean."

Coble pondered the new information a moment. Was it useful? He didn't have a clue. "Okay. Thanks."

———

THE OLD KEY was simply window-dressing and didn't fit the lock. Looking at the door, Coble doubted any key would have turned the rusty tumblers. He was surprised the door opened easily with hardly a squeak. Once inside, number fourteen looked the same as most other frontier hotel rooms, although this one was at least clean. He didn't see any bugs running around or spiders spinning in the corners. Maybe there wouldn't be any.

One window decorated the room, complete with faded curtains. The single, iron-railed bed perpendicular to it. A washstand held a basin and porcelain pitcher, both etched with blue flowers. He looked in the pitcher, didn't see anything foreign floating about, so it was probably all right. Two towels were stacked on the top of the counter. The closet consisted of several nails driven into the wall by the door.

He stripped off his shirt and tossed it on the bed. His hat followed, and then his gun belt. Pouring water into the basin, he soaked a towel and removed the sweat and dirt of several days' travel. Tomorrow, he'd have to find a bath.

A board creaked outside his door. Close after came a soft knock. Before he could get to the door, the knocking became more insistent. He drew one of his pistols, and with his left hand, opened the door.

"I really don't think the gun will be necessary, Coble."

Jessica stood in the hall and stared at him from the depths of dark blue eyes you could get lost in if you weren't careful.

"Well?" Her voice was low and throaty. "Cat got your tongue?"

He stood in front of the entryway. Not that he could lay claim to being the most moral person in the world, but this just wasn't done in polite circles.

He shook himself free from overthinking the situation. "Is there something I can do for you?"

She started to come through the doorway, then abruptly stopped when she ran into him. "The first thing you can do is get me out of the hallway. I don't want the whole town knowing I visited your room."

He smiled at her. "You haven't, yet."

She stepped past him, moving his gun aside with her hand. When he just stood there watching her, she returned and closed the door. "You're starting to act a little backward, Coble."

Turning, she picked up his shirt and handed it to him, then sat on the edge of the bed. Even under her slight weight, the bed sagged. Maybe he'd sleep on the floor.

She continued. "That's a nasty little scratch on your side. You should be more careful riding the trails."

He looked at her a long moment, trying to see if she were joking. "It's a bullet wound. And I'm lucky it's only a scratch. By the way, didn't I leave you at your house?"

She chuckled and bounced on the bed. "You'll find I don't always stay where people put me, or do what they tell me to do. Besides, the house seemed empty after you left. Curious, don't you think?"

She looked around the room. "I think these rooms are all the same. Mine is down the hall, if you're wondering."

"I wasn't." He slipped on his shirt, ignoring her staring at his chest—well, as best he could. "Do you stay in town often? Seems a needless expense, with you living so close."

She sighed, looking out the window. "Truth is, since my daughter's death, I do stay in town quite often."

He leaned against the doorframe, arms folded across his chest. "What's this all about, Jess?"

"Jess." She thought a moment after repeating her name. "I think I like that. From you anyway. And I'm here because I'm going to help you find the killer."

He came away from the wall. "Now, wait a minute."

"I've thought about it and decided it's the best course of action to take."

He couldn't believe his ears. "You...thought about it."

"Yes. There's nothing left for me at the ranch. The few chores I have can be done by a neighbor.

Actually, I think he wants to buy me out. I just might let him."

Coble shook his head, thought about it, and then shook it again. "Your helping me is the very worst idea I've ever heard. I work alone, and it's damned dangerous."

Her voice was pleading. "I need this, and I'm hoping you'll understand. Please. The waiting is killing me. I can't stand not doing anything."

"Look. I'm sorry. But your daughter is gone. Dead and buried. All that's left for you to do is get on with your life the best you can."

"You're not listening to me. I'm going to help."

He tried another tact. "I figured to catch up with Caleb. He'll know the best way to proceed."

"He'll find you when he needs you. Look, I know the country as well as he does. I can help you, if you allow me to." She got up and moved to the door. As she passed close by him, she said in a soft voice, "Did you draw that pistol to shoot someone? Didn't you say that's the only reason to have it?"

His level gaze met hers. "I haven't decided on that yet. I'm kinda leaning toward pulling the trigger."

"Well, don't go off by accident." She patted him on the chest, hand lingering a moment, and then gave him a slow smile. "Daybreak?"

Then she was gone, except for a lingering scent of jasmine mixed with...woman?

"Dammit." He stood staring at the door, gun in

hand, but nothing changed. She didn't come back, and daybreak was getting closer. Not liking the sound of it the first time, he put more feeling into it.

"*Dammit!*"

Chapter Ten

AFTER JESSICA LEFT, COBLE STOOD BY THE DOOR, listening. She walked down the hall, then opened a door and closed it softly.

She was close, then. He smiled, thinking about her. That would be nice. Maybe.

No sooner than he started to take his shirt off again, there came another knock on the door. Still smiling, and with all the wrong expectations, he opened the door.

It was his night for women.

He gazed at the girl standing in the doorway. Beautiful women.

She was the complete opposite of Jessica Davis. Medium height, with long, jet-black hair and snapping black eyes that spoke of Spanish Conquistadors and faraway kings, ladies in waiting, and matters of court. Though dressed in jeans and a plaid cotton shirt, she wore them like she was on the ballroom floor. Her hat hung down her back by a leather string, and she held a riding quirt, absent-mindedly slapping it on the palm of her hand.

"You are Coble Bray." It came as a statement, not a question. Her gaze was steady on his. How could he get so lucky?

"Well, if I wasn't before, I certainly am now." He looked up and down the hall. "Is there a whole line of women out here just waiting to see me?"

She looked at him just long enough to let him know he wasn't nearly as funny as he thought.

"Pete sent me." Her voice was low and husky, softer than he'd ever heard a woman speak, and he leaned toward her to hear better. "He wants you to come right away."

"Where?" He tried to look down the hall to see if Pete were around. She watched him like he might try to get away. The thought didn't seem too much out of the question.

"He is out in the hills, a few miles south of here. I will take you to him."

"At night? Young lady, it's pitch black out there. Besides, it's been a long day. I'm tired and had no supper. I'll see Pete in the morning."

The girl stood with her hands on her hips. Her lips thinned down and her black eyes got even blacker. "Are you always this obstinate?"

"Nope. It gets worse. Look, I'm just a man who likes his sleep. How do you know Pete?"

"Ask him yourself." An exasperated sound came from deep in her throat. "If we leave now, we'll be there by sunup."

He smiled at her. "Or..." He stretched the word out. "Here's a better idea. If I go to sleep now, I'll be fresh as a daisy at sunup and ready to face all the new problems of the day."

When he didn't move, she slapped her quirt against her jeans. "Look, Pete found the body of a young girl. He said to tell you it's fresh. There might be a trail."

He looked at her a moment, trying to read the expression in her eyes. Familiar eyes, but he couldn't fathom why. Suddenly all business, he turned immediately and began stuffing his shirt in his pants.

"I'll be ready in a minute. Why don't you go get the sheriff?"

When he didn't hear her move, he slowly turned back around, eyebrows raised.

She leaned tiredly against the doorframe. "Pete thought you should see this one before anyone else."

He thought about that a moment and then, with a sigh, strapped on his gun belt. "All right, then. Let's go get my horse."

She just shook her head at him. "It's already saddled. He doesn't take to a halter any better than you." She rubbed her arm. "And he bites."

A grim smile spread his lips. "Well, now. You've learned a lesson today. Let's go see Pete."

———

As THEY LEFT TOWN, the girl gave instructions to the hostler at the stable to rouse the sheriff at dawn and send him south on the trail. She assured the hostler they would be easy to find.

The trail was dark, dimly lit by a waning moon, with branches whipping their faces and a cacophony of insects and tree frogs serenading them. They traveled slowly, by need more than choice. Even at the slow rate of travel, it would be easy to lose their way.

He broke the silence as they stopped a moment to rest their horses and get their bearings. "So, what's your name?"

"Maria."

"Maria." He repeated it, trying to burn it into his memory. "Got a last name, Maria?"

She urged her horse forward abruptly. "Yes."

Maria rode slowly, stopping often to look for some sign of where they were. He thought he could see well at night but vowed to himself never to let this girl hunt him after the sun went down. Watching her back and the lithe, relaxed grace with which she guided the horse, he thought of the girls down Sonora way, south of the border. A curious combination of Spanish, Indian, and roving Texans that bred women who were beautiful at an early age, then turned prematurely old by wind, sun, and Apache raids. And the occasional exceptions like Maria, who seemed to wear her beauty in defiance of all these things.

As dawn sent fingers of light through the trees and the eastern sky turned a brassy gold, she abruptly left the trail. He followed, and within minutes, Pete

Santos stepped out from behind an elderberry clump, brushing off his pants. Coble started to speak but, noting the expression on Pete's face, stopped in mid-word. He glanced at the girl and the thought came unbidden to his mind, totally out of place. Her beauty stunned him. The morning light moved across her face and highlighted her eyes. Eyes that now held steadily on his, waiting for some action from him.

Sighing, he turned back to Pete. "So, tell me what you've found."

"Not much to tell. We were looking for a place to camp. I smelled smoke, so we turned off the trail into this clearing."

"We?" He remembered their conversation at the train station and looked back and forth between them. "The relative?"

Pete gave him a pointed look, cleared his throat, and nodded at Maria. "She saw the body first. I've never seen anything like it. Anyway, I told her to stay away and went to look it over. Then I sent her to look for you. Thought you would want to look things over before anyone else got here to mess up the sign."

"You smelled smoke? A lot of smoke, like a signal fire, or just a hint?"

When no answer came, he looked into Pete's eyes. He didn't see what he expected. He expected to see anger in his expression, but all he could read was pain. He expected to see satisfaction, however fleeting, for finding the body, but all he saw was bewilderment and loathing. He glanced over Pete's shoulder toward the stark white object in the middle of the clearing.

"You could have covered her."

"No, I couldn't. I ain't going back in there. I've seen some spooky things in my life and more dead people than I like to think about, but nothing like this."

"Couldn't be any worse than what the Comanche did to that settler family we run on to last year, down on the Cimarron."

"Oh, we've seen people used up worse, that's for damn sure. But this is just...different."

He thought about that a moment, finding himself curiously reluctant to proceed and he couldn't really put a finger on the why of it. When he glanced around, both Pete and the girl watched him, waiting. As he looked at Maria, one of her eyebrows raised slightly as if to say get on with it.

He took a big breath, letting the air out slowly. "All right. Where have you walked?"

"Are you stalling, Mr. Bray?" Maria's voice was mocking.

"Quiet, girl." Pete's voice was sharp. "Quit digging at him."

Pete continued. "I walked up on her left side. Straight. From here to there and back. That's the only tracks of mine you'll see."

"And Maria didn't go over there?"

"I can answer for myself." Her voice was quiet

but forceful. "No, I didn't go over there. Pete wouldn't let me."

He looked askance at her. "Tell me, in another life, did I kick you in the shins? Hurt you in some way? Some affront I know nothing about?"

She started to speak, then closed her mouth and settled into her saddle. Ignoring her then, he dismounted and handed the reins to Pete, shucking the blanket from behind the saddle and draping it over his shoulder. "Sit tight. I'll look around."

Ignoring the body, he walked the perimeter of the clearing, an opening in the forest resembling a small room. The surrounding brush and foliage looked almost solid. The glade probably had direct sunlight for a couple of hours around noon, but it was enough to grow a lush amount of grass. Judging by the tracks, deer kept the grass cropped short like a manicured lawn.

Each time he passed the others, his circle became smaller. At one point, farthest from Pete and Maria and on the other side of the clearing, he dropped his hat on the ground.

Maria turned to Pete, but the question froze on her lips when he held his hand up signaling for quiet. She let out a gusty sigh, folded her arms across her chest, and turned back to watch.

He circled the clearing, cataloging everything he thought was useful. Finally, he stopped at the body.

She was young, with long brown hair braided in a V down her back, turned dark with dirt and blood. Her hands were tied behind her with a strip of rawhide that had cut deeply into her skin, and she kneeled with her forehead against the ground.

If her hands were out in front of her, she would have looked like a vassal genuflecting to her king.

Her throat was cut while in that position and she'd bled out right there. She hadn't struggled, either. Judging by the number of bruises and scratches on her skin, he wondered if the end was merciful for her. Mottled bruising was evident on her shoulders and buttocks, and blood where none should be. From the looks of it, she had been gripped hard, maybe raped. He reached out his hand to cover one set of bruises.

Soft steps and a barely audible "My god" told him curiosity got the best of Maria.

"What kind of animal would murder a young girl like this?" She spoke in a near whisper.

He shook his head, gazing at the forest and then back to the body. "The meanest animal of all. Man. And it's not just a murder. It's more like a sacrifice. Some kind of ritual, maybe. See this set of bruises? Put your hand over them, a fingertip for each bruise."

She did, not quite touching the girl, and the stretch of her hand was just smaller than the bruises.

"If that is a handprint," she said. "And the killer is a man. He must have small hands." Taking his hand, she put hers against his, palm to palm, and his hand dwarfed hers.

He pointed in the direction the girl kneeled. "Someone made a cross out of grapevines."

"Is it a cross or a headstone?" she asked.

"I don't know, but it's a good point. Shows you're thinking." And it did. He was impressed with her poise. It was better than his. He continued, as if talking to himself, "You'd make a fine investigator the way you think."

She glanced at him quickly, and he thought she looked startled.

He looked down at the murdered girl, then took his gaze away and glanced around the clearing. Even though the sun was fully up, the space around them still dwelled in shadows. He looked at the grapevine cross, directly in line with the murdered girl's head, maybe fifteen feet away. Then he looked behind her.

"I am not an expert like you..."

He glanced at her but didn't see any sign of derision.

"But," she continued. "I don't see any tracks or anything. It's like she dropped from the sky."

He shook his head. "Hardly. There's nothing supernatural about this. It's just plain old murder. Whoever did this took a broken branch and broomed the place. You can see the brush marks in some of the grass."

"I still don't see it."

He leaned over and pointed to several places in the grass. "It's been a while, and most of the grass has straightened, but some of the grass is broken.

See? Some pushed left. Some right. Like sweeping a floor."

"Coincidence?"

"Maybe?" He shrugged. "Doubt it."

Maria held her hand out to him, and after a moment of hesitation, wondering what she wanted, he gave her the blanket. Holding one end, she rolled it out and then covered the girl's body.

He cocked his head and listened for a moment, then spoke to Pete. "Let's walk the horses around the edge of the clearing to the other side, Pete. We got company."

"I hear them. We better skedaddle out of here."

"No. You stay. Tell the sheriff just what you found and how you found it. His name is Stiles. You were passing through. Don't mention me unless you get cornered."

Pete hesitated. "You said Stiles? Where's Caleb?"

"No time. We'll talk later."

"Where will you be?"

Coble moved toward his hat. "Found a piece of a track. I think I'll see where it goes."

———

MARIA GLANCED at Pete and then at the retreating back of Coble Bray. "Wait up, Marshal. I'm coming, too."

"Good. You can lead the horses."

She started to protest, but he was already concentrating on the solitary track he'd found. As she watched, change came over him. He became quiet and withdrawn, appearing single-minded as a wolf on a trail, moving through the brush surrounding the clearing. Grabbing up the reins of their horses, slapping Red on the nose just to get her bluff in, she followed close behind.

Maria watched, mesmerized as he worked out the trail. The change she'd seen come over him in Kansas City had happened again. Somehow, he appeared colder. When he glanced at her, he looked right through her. Any hint of humor was gone, and she realized it was a mask he hid behind.

He held his gaze to the ground like a hawk following a mouse through the grass. Every few feet he would point to something—a bent clump of grass, a broken twig on a bush, a rock turned over, or a depression in the ground where none should be. In the space of a few moments, she learned more about working a trail than the sum of everything Pete tried to teach her.

Within a few minutes, he stopped. She tied the horses to a sapling and approached quietly behind him, alarmed when she saw him draw his Colt.

"What is it?" she whispered.

His voice was soft, barely audible. "Something is not right."

"Like...?"

He held his hand up, silencing her. Once she was quiet a moment, she felt it too. No sound. Not a bird chirping or squirrel barking. Even the breeze failed to move the leaves of the trees. She shivered from a sudden chill.

Then, as if waking from a dream, the feeling disappeared.

Facing the forest, he holstered his weapon. "Well, whoever it was, he's gone."

He kneeled by a smoothed-off patch of ground. "Maria, what do you make of this?"

There was a drawing in the dirt, with something printed at the bottom. "Looks like someone drew a snake then wrote the words I AM under the tail." He took his hat off and ran his hand through his hair. "We were led to this spot. How could he know we'd find the trail? Did he expect a tracker?"

"Look fresh, like it was just done..." Her voice trailed off to nothing.

His sharp gaze lingered on her pensive expression. "What is it?"

"What? Oh, nothing. Just remembering a Bible passage. What do you make of the drawing?"

"Seems simple enough. Sign of the snake. Indians use it some. It's supposed to bring them luck. I don't remember what kind."

"And the words?" she asked.

Coble sighed, glancing around at the trees and brush. "Beats the hell out of me. Maybe *I am a snake* is the message."

"Don't get testy, Marshal."

He turned to her abruptly, pinning her with his gaze. "Who are you?" Exactly?

She didn't bat an eye at the change of subject. "Maria Santos."

His face was a study as she watched him work through it. She knew Pete told him he had to meet with a relative and wouldn't tell Coble who or where.

"I'm his daughter." She finally offered an explanation.

"Didn't know he had one. Your mother must have been one hell of a beautiful woman."

Her cheeks warmed. "I understand that she was. She died when I was born. But thank you."

As they talked, he'd moved closer to her, and she could feel the animal magnetism radiating from him, could feel the same thing she'd felt the first time she saw him. Looking up into his eyes, she knew he felt it, too. His gray eyes seemed to miss nothing, and his expression was soft as he watched her, and the laughter was back. With her gaze on his smile, her hand gentle on his arm, her lips parted slightly, she started up on her tiptoes, leaning forward...

He abruptly stepped away from her. "We'd better get back to town. There are some people I need to talk to."

He brushed by her to get the horses. Flustered by her own actions, she could only stare at his back and wonder. Had he missed the signals? Was he blind? How many men would pass up a chance to kiss a pretty girl alone in the woods? Then, as if cold water was thrown on her, she thought of what they'd seen just minutes before and blushed, softly cursing at herself. How could she have forgotten that? And worse, what would he think of her, throwing herself at him like that?

Sitting his horse and handing the reins of her mount to her, he asked, "What was the verse?"

Still flustered, her answer was sharper than intended. "What?"

"The Bible verse. What was it?"

"Oh. I don't remember all of it. I think it was in Exodus. When Moses asked God who he should say had sent him. God replied I Am." She thought a moment. "I think."

"You think?" He chuckled. "Great. Nothing like being sure. You coming?"

She balked a moment. "It could be a clue or insight on why this was done." When he didn't answer, she mumbled. "Well, it could."

———

A FEW MINUTES LATER, they rode single file on a trail Coble assumed went back to town. At least, it was meandering in the right direction. The trail widened going through a glade and he pulled to the side, allowing Maria to move her horse next to him.

"Don't put too much stock in that message."

"But why?" she asked. "We need to understand why he's doing this. If we do that, we have a better idea who to look for. Correct?"

He shook his head. "It's a red herring."

"I don't know the term." Her voice held a contrived innocence. "Isn't a herring a fish?"

He chuckled. "Sure you don't. It's a distraction, college girl. What did they teach you in that school?"

She glanced at him a moment. "Well, I kind of never went to that college. I mean...I tried, but it was dull as a box of rocks. The girls were stuck up with all the attention span of a flock of birds. All they could talk about—"

His gaze was sharp as he interrupted. "What about Pete? He's bust-a-gut proud of you going to college."

"I'm sorry about that." She sighed. "I meant to tell him, but just never had the guts to do it. If it is any consolation, with all the money he sent me, I have saved a nice little nest egg for his retirement."

He laughed at this. Pete had a pretty good nest egg already. They had grubstaked a prospector a few years ago. It had turned out well and the man was grateful and honest.

"If you are through laughing at me, why is the writing a distraction? The message was left for a purpose."

He reined in his horse and looked at her. "It's a distraction because it doesn't matter. Why he did it only matters to the killer. It does not matter to me. Any message will be lost. What does matter is that he must be stopped. His executioner won't care about the nuances of the message."

Glancing at her, he said, "You know that word? Nuance?"

She gave him a skin-stripping look. "Yes. I know the word. So, how can you find this man?"

"Oh, I'm thinking it won't be very hard. If you look in a box of snakes, it is not hard to pick out the rattler."

"What if you can't tell? What if he doesn't allow himself to be seen?"

"This is a small community. He'll be seen. And I'm thinking this snake will try and bite if I get too close. I'm sure of it."

"So, you're counting on him trying to kill you?"

Coble shrugged. "It happens."

Chapter Eleven

THE TRIP BACK TO TOWN WAS UNEVENTFUL. AFTER their short conversation, Coble was lost in thought and Maria didn't disturb him. At the edge of town, she reined in her horse, saying she'd wait for Pete.

Looking at her, he said, "Be careful."

She snorted. "I think I'm too old for this killer."

He gave a slight hand wave and cantered off into town. The sun was climbing above the hills, casting shadows into the street as he rode to the front of the hotel. He needed answers and this was the quickest way.

"Is Mrs. Davis in her room?"

The clerk behind the hotel desk barely looked up from his ledger, just pointed upstairs.

Coble sighed. "Mind telling me which room?"

The man gave him a startled look. "Sorry, I thought everyone knew by now. It's room six."

"Why would I know her room number?"

The clerk colored slightly and shrugged, then

went back to his writing. "There have been quite a few visitors lately. I made a wrong assumption."

Walking down the hall toward room six, he caught a fleeting glimpse of a door closing at the end of the hall. Knowing that door went to the back stairs, he paused a moment, thinking about it. A completely normal happening, but something tickled his brain. She gets a lot of visitors?

Shrugging and chiding himself to mind his own business, he turned and knocked on Mrs. Davis's door. When she answered, he spoke quietly. "May I talk to you a minute, ma'am?"

After a startled glance at him, she backed away and indicated an empty chair. She looked a little flustered, and kept pushing at hair that seemed to be unruly. The room smelled like there'd been a morning rain of lilac water.

"You look like the bearer of bad news. You also missed our date this morning at daybreak."

He shook his head. "You made that date, not me. Pardon me if I seem abrupt, but all hell is about to break loose as soon as the sheriff gets back to town. There was a body found this morning. Another young girl."

"Dear God."

"I'm sorry, but there are some questions I'd like to ask about your daughter. It's very personal, so I'll understand if you send me away."

"I'll do whatever I can to help. I told you that." She raised her chin and seemed to steel herself.

"Captain Meyers found the body of your daughter?"

"Yes." Her voice broke.

He hesitated a moment. "I'm sorry. I know this must be hard."

She tried to gain control of herself. "Why is this important?"

He looked closely at her. "If I can be assured you will keep this in confidence, ma'am?"

"I'm not in the habit of running around telling stories or gossiping, especially where the memory of my daughter is concerned."

"All right. The girl we found this morning died in a very distinctive way. I'm just wondering if there are any similarities between how she was found and your daughter."

"How?" She paused, shaking her head. "What was done?"

He sighed, wishing he had a shot of whiskey to take the bad taste out of his mouth. "The girl was kneeling toward a crude homemade cross." He purposefully didn't mention his suspicion of rape. "I found some writing nearby that may be a Bible verse."

She shook her head, frowning. "That's...odd. I didn't see my daughter until they brought her in. I really wish I could help. Caleb didn't mention anything about it though, and I think he would have. Maybe the new sheriff will know."

"I doubt it, but he's next on my list."

"Then I wish you luck." Anger crept into her

voice. "Please inform me if you have any news. I meant what I said at our first meeting. No stone will be left unturned until the killer is found. I'm taking steps to make sure that happens. Sitting idle isn't my way, and I've waited too long now."

"What have you done?" He gave her a wary glance.

She answered defensively. "Since you don't seem to want my assistance, I have hired someone else to investigate."

"Who?"

She was standing and patting her foot nervously. "A man came to me highly recommended. A Mr. Perez."

"Onofrio?" Knowing the man's reputation, Coble was confused. "Who in the world would recommend him?"

She looked at him doubtfully. "The new sheriff. Why? You don't approve?"

"Onofrio Perez is a killer for hire. He'd be more likely to be the culprit than help find your daughter's killer."

Her eyes blazed. "And just exactly how does that make him different than you?"

Well now. With a sigh, he stood abruptly, placing his hat back on his head. "You sent for me, Mrs. Davis. I didn't ask to come. I've been here two days and somehow I'm not moving fast enough so you replace me with a hired killer?"

He shook his head. "Have you known Pop Janus long?"

She gave him a startled glance. "Since I was a young girl."

"All right. If you trust him, ask him about Perez. Or ask Caleb when you see him, or Captain Meyers." He was getting angrier with each word. "Or, hell. Ask any ten-year-old you find on the street. They'll tell you about Onofrio Perez."

He paused a moment, trying to overcome his anger. "It sounds to me like you just want someone dead in retribution and don't care who it is. Don't let your daughter's death do that to you." He stared into her shocked and angry eyes and then tipped his hat to her. "Good day to you, Mrs. Davis. Guess I'd better go turn some rocks over. Hopefully, I won't find your new investigator under one."

————

WALKING OUT OF THE HOTEL, Coble ran into Captain Meyers. Talking to the man, he was still impressed with his demeanor and frank answers to questions. He liked people who were direct, so he decided to take a chance.

"Captain, I need a favor."

"Of course, Marshal. Whatever I can do."

"Mrs. Davis is getting herself into something I'm not sure she can handle. I know she's upset at the loss of her daughter, and she's really upset that I haven't found the killer in the one and a half days I've been here." He shared a smile with Meyers at that. "I can't be everywhere at once, Captain. I could use some help where she's concerned."

"What kind of help?" he asked with a smile. "You should know that Jessica and I have been walking out some, and I intend to continue meeting with her. Understand, I'm trying to make things a lot more serious between us." He grinned again. "I hope you're not trying to enlist my help to further your own plans."

Coble looked at Meyers a moment, then shook his head ruefully. "Far from it. I just got here. I admit there might be some interest on both our parts, but that is not what I need. And things may not be as they seem with Mrs. Davis."

Meyers held up his hand to forestall any more comments. "I'm aware of some of Jessica's...proclivities, shall we say? Doesn't matter to me. So, the favor?"

"I was just up in her hotel room." Meyers lost his smile quickly and Coble held his hand up to stop the inevitable question. "She told me that you found her daughter. Was there anything strange about the body when you found it?"

Meyers lost his humor. "She was naked and had her hands tied behind her back. We found her on her side, but there was dirt and leaves stuck to her knees, so I'm thinking she was kneeling and then fell over. I'm sorry, but I didn't pay a lot of attention. As soon as we found her and I could see she was dead, I covered her and sent a rider for Caleb. Why?"

"We found another girl this morning, killed in the same manner. This is getting very strange."

Meyers stood, looking into the distance. Finally he spoke. "I'm sure we've seen more death than either of us wants to remember. But this? I don't understand it."

"I told someone earlier not to try and overthink this. A bear or wolf will kill when it's hungry. A big cat kills because it can and wants to. It's simple. Predators kill. Animal or human. There's not much to understand. We just need to stop it." Coble caught the captain's gaze. "Oh, one more mystery. Your Mrs. Davis informed me that she's tired of waiting on me and has hired someone to assist in the investigation."

"What? Who?"

"Onofrio Perez."

The language of a line officer and someone used to the rough and tumble life on the frontier can often be colorful and to the point. After listening to a couple of minutes of this, he held up his hand to silence Meyers.

"It appears you know his reputation. Watch out for her. And, Captain? I'm not in your way on that account. One more thing? I notice you're not wearing a sidearm."

Meyers looked grimly at him. "I will remedy that situation immediately."

Coble remembered thinking that he wouldn't like to see those eyes looking at him over a gun barrel. If possible, Meyers's eyes became even more cold-looking.

"You can also cross Perez off your list of worries," Meyers said. "He will not be assisting Jessica and is not your worry any longer."

The two men shook hands.

"Thanks, Captain. Once he knows you're on to him, you'll need to watch your back." He hoped the soldier wouldn't bite off more than he could chew. Perez was known to be fast with his gun and not too choosy about fair play.

————

COBLE STRADDLED a ladder-back wicker chair under the awning of the sheriff's porch as he watched the small cavalcade of riders come into town. His anger at Jessica dissipated as the buckboard carrying the body of the girl stopped at the undertaker's building while the men on horseback continued up the street. Most went directly to the saloon. The sheriff and his deputies turned in at the jail.

As they trooped up the steps, he stood and stepped between the sheriff and his men. "I'll be speaking to the sheriff alone, gents."

The men stood milling around a moment, waiting for some direction from the sheriff. They didn't like being told what to do, but also didn't want to cross a mad-looking deputy United States marshal.

"Y'all go on," the sheriff finally said. "And no

talking about this, you hear me?" His voice faded to barely audible as he went into the office. "We got enough problems."

After they went inside, Coble closed the door behind him. "Your deputies may not talk, but you know the rest of them are at it already, over at the saloon. You want to tell me about some of those other problems?"

Not answering, Stiles sat heavily in his chair with a gusty sigh. Hands flat on the desktop, he paused a moment, then reached down and opened a drawer. Pulling out a bottle of whiskey and a couple of glasses, he raised one to Coble.

"No thanks. It's a little early for me."

"Me too." Stiles poured three fingers of the amber liquid into the glass. The sheriff downed the drink and then proceeded to knock down two more just like it. "Hell of a way to start the day."

"It is that." Coble pulled a chair up next to the desk and sat down. "Do you still think you have everything under control?"

The man stared at him and then poured another drink.

Coble shook his head. "Keep that up and you won't last till noon."

"Good."

He decided to talk before the man was dead drunk. "Did anyone talk to the people who found the Davis girl?"

"This another interrogation, Marshal?"

"If it needs to be. Did you?"

"Sure, I was the deputy then. I went along with McGill." Stiles's answer came low-voiced, his manner dejected.

"Did she look the same as the girl this morning, or I should say presented the same?" Even though he'd talked to Captain Meyers, he was still trying to get a handle on how the girls were killed. Maybe that would tell him why. Though he'd discounted it to Maria, he really did need to know.

"From what they said, yeah. About the same," Stiles admitted.

He bored into Stiles. "Then you have two killings. Both done and presented the same way. This isn't going away, even with your old scalp to wave around."

"A problem?" Stiles replied in a shaky voice. He was pale and gray as three days dead, even after the shots of whiskey. The sheriff continued in a slurred voice. "You don't know the half of it."

"Then spell it out for me. What's going on around here? What don't I know?"

Stiles gave a soundless laugh as he downed another shot. "It's four killings, Marshal. Jenny Slocum. Her folks' farm some bottomland just north of here. Then there's Faith James."

"James?"

"Yeah, James. With everything that name implies. I've got every border jumper and holdup artist in four counties riding the trails looking for who knows what. In a couple of cases, if they didn't find something, they just made it up. You know about Elaine Davis. She was the third, at least that we know of."

Stiles shook his head. "Christ, what a mess this is. Now, there's Isabel Jakes. And that may be the worst problem of all. Her father's Isaiah Jakes. He moved here from the high up hills in Tennessee and knows nothing but the Bible and hardscrabble work. His people are Old Testament Bible thumpers. People will start dying for this, and he is not going to be too choosy about who it is. Four girls. They were all young, and they all died with their throats cut. McGill didn't have a damned clue about the killer and I don't either."

Coble sat staring at the wall a moment, and when he could finally find his voice, he asked. "Was the Davis girl scalped?"

Stiles's head jerked up, and he looked at Coble a moment and finally conceded. "No. Nothing like that."

"Any of the others? Were they scalped?" Coble asked quietly.

"No, dammit. Does that satisfy you?"

He shook his head, thinking of the judge and his desire for a quick settlement. "No, somehow it doesn't."

The sheriff looked at him a moment, then returned to his glass.

"Did you find anything unusual with the bodies?" Coble continued. "Or was anything turned in?"

"You mean other than them being sliced up,

and..." Stiles gave his whiskey glass closer scrutiny. "No. Nothing else."

The man dropped his gaze back to the table, apparently giving in to the effects of the whiskey. Coble just stared at him until the sheriff finally raised his eyes and returned his look.

"Thanks for the help, Sheriff. I'll let myself out." With his hand on the latch, he turned. "The Indian you took the scalp from...the scalp you were trying to pass as the girl's? That was murder. When this is done, I'll be around to see you about that."

Stiles gave him a cold smile. "You would have to prove that."

"Only to myself. And you've already confessed."

Chapter Twelve

COBLE STEPPED OUT OF THE SHERIFF'S OFFICE DEEP in thought about the murders and what kind of animal would do this to people—and as he'd told Maria...the human kind. The question was, which human was it and how to find him.

A glint of reflected light pulled his attention to the right and he saw two men on horseback with guns pointed right at him. They were grinning, and in the quiet morning air, he distinctly heard them ear back the hammers on their pistols.

Even as he registered the sound, he was moving. With an oath, he lurched to one side. The first shots missed, the bullets thudding into the wall beside him.

At the same time, gunshots erupted from inside the bank, a few doors down the walk. Amid the thunder and powder smoke, he dove forward to the street, drawing his guns as he went down. A bullet passed between his arm and side, cutting through his shirt and leaving a burning slice. Another bullet skinned the side of his neck as he rolled hard in the mud.

As he came up firing, men ran from the bank and mounted in a tight knot of plunging horses, men in long coats and pullover masks.

Gun smoke puff-balled around them as the robbers reined around to face the street, each man facing a different direction. With military precision.

He knew these boys.

Two more men ran out of the bank, one carrying a heavy gunnysack, and leaped on their horses.

He kneeled by the hitch rail and traded shots with one of the riders. Both men missed, and he had to roll away again as the wooden rail beside him erupted in splinters. Both guns were empty and he didn't remember firing more than twice. Frantically, he rolled toward the cover of the plank walk as he searched his pockets for the loaded cylinders he carried.

"Marshal!"

He turned toward the sheriff's door as a shotgun sailed through the air toward him. Catching the gun, he whirled and, rocking back both hammers, pulled both triggers of the double-barrel at once, hoping to clear out the group of riders firing at him, but the riders had spread out and were moving quickly away. One man screamed as his slicker spurted red, and he grabbed his saddle horn to keep from falling off his horse. Another rider crowded close to the wounded man to support him as they thundered off down the street.

One of the riders threw his arms out, his rifle flying toward the boardwalk, and then dropped from his horse before the sound of a rifle firing from the other end of the street registered. Maria and Pete rode hard toward him, both standing in their stirrups, cavalry style, firing rifles at the retreating bandits. They pulled up between him and the gang of robbers and watched them sweep around a corner at the end of the street and into the forest beyond.

Standing in the street with the empty shotgun in one hand and an empty revolver in the other, he took a deep breath, trying to control his slamming nerves and breathing. His hat was gone and a trickle of blood ran down over one eye. The neck wound stung with sweat and mud. He looked down at himself and saw a hole in his shirt, another in his pant cuff, and blood dripping on his boots.

"Well, now." He smiled at Maria as she dismounted, leaping from her horse, hoping she wouldn't see how dazed he felt. "That was like the circus came to town."

"What in hell were you thinking, walking into a holdup like that?" Maria's hands poked and prodded on him to see if he was hurt. "If we could see what was going on from the end of the street, you should have caught on from fifty feet away. You were right in the middle of it."

People slowly edged out of doors, looking at the dead man lying in a heap at the end of the street and then running toward the bank. Inside the bank, someone shouted for a doctor, and the sound of more running and yelling started.

Before he could answer her questions, the sheriff stepped out of his office and onto the porch, heading for the bank next door.

Coble called. "Thanks for the loan of the gun, Sheriff."

The sheriff finger-waggled a wave at him as he staggered toward the bank.

He stood in the street, dripping blood and dirt as Maria made circles around him. He lifted his gaze to Pete, who still sat slouched in his saddle. "I didn't hear any shots coming from the jail."

"Me, neither." Pete stared into the bank. "Not a one. I can't figure why he tossed you the Greener."

"Professional courtesy?"

Pete snorted. "Doubt it."

"He's drunk, so who knows." He looked at Pete soberly. "Thanks for the help."

"It wasn't just us. That Army captain was laying into them, too."

Meyers? Hadn't taken him long to get armed.

Somehow that pleased him. He grabbed Maria by the arm. "Stop circling around me like a flock of buzzards."

Maria's grip on his arm was more painful than his wounds as she shook him with each spaced-out word. "You could have been killed."

He looked at her. "Every damned day. Pete, we'd better meet up in my room, pronto. The way Maria is fussin' and cluckin', she's going to lay an egg soon, and that would be a poor sight to see right out here on the street."

———

THE TENSION in room fourteen of the Commercial Hotel was palpable. At least for Coble. Pete told them he'd be up later. He had to run an errand first, leaving Coble and Maria alone. He sat on the bed stripped to the waist. She pulled the wash table closer and cleaned the mud from his wounds. She stood in front of him, straddling one of his legs as she washed the scalp wound. When she was finished pushing and prodding, then finally cleaning the wound to her satisfaction, she stood pressing a cloth against it to stop the fresh bleeding.

"Head wounds are so messy. You are very lucky."

"My hat wasn't. It won't keep the rain out now."

"This is not funny. You came very close to being as dead as your hat. I cannot imagine what you were thinking." She paused a moment, a ghost of a smile on her lips. "Maybe your mind was on a young and beautiful woman, hmm?"

Maria wore a riding skirt and a soft gingham blouse that had somehow become unbuttoned enough to show the swell of her breasts. With her chest just inches from his nose and her warm fragrance surrounding him, he found it hard to concentrate. She kept finding ways to reach around his head for something and lean even closer, accidentally bumping him on occasion. He started to comment on it when the door to the room abruptly opened.

The sight of Coble and Maria so close together arrested Jessica's entrance.

Her observation was instant and sharp. "My, how cozy."

Startled, he started to rise but couldn't get past Maria's legs.

With one hand on his shoulder and the other still holding a pad of cloth on his head, Maria used her body to push him back to a sitting position.

"Sit still. You will start bleeding again." She turned to Jessica. "Have you ever heard of knocking?"

A fire built in Maria as Jessica came on into the room, a slow, mocking smile forming.

Placing his hands firmly on Maria's hips, he moved her aside and grabbed his shirt.

"Stand at ease, Mr. Bray," Jessica said. "I've seen you without a shirt before, remember?"

He ignored her advice and pulled on his shirt. "May I do something for you?"

"When?" Maria swiveled her head between the two of them. "When was this?"

"Well, when he was at my house changing clothes, of course." Jessica smiled at her and then turned back to him. "I heard you'd been shot and came to check on you. I was concerned." She paused. "It looks like the situation is well in hand, so to speak."

Maria started to advance on the other woman with a low growl, but he stepped into her path. "It's nothing serious. Just a few scratches."

He was busy blocking Maria. "Have you two met? Mrs. Davis, this is Maria Santos. She's the daughter of a close friend of mine. Maria, this is Jessica Davis. Her daughter was killed a few weeks ago. I'm here partly because she wrote me a letter asking me to come."

Maria turned very pale, looking at Jessica a moment. With a sigh, she stepped around Coble and offered her hand. "I'm sorry for your loss. It must be a terrible thing."

"It is terrible. Actually, it's mind-numbing." Jessica shrugged. "I'm sorry, too. It seems I'm very snippy lately. I was just surprised to find a young girl alone in the same room with a man."

"You mean this particular man, do you not?" Maria immediately rose to the challenge. Her voice was innocently sweet. "It looks to me like you had the same thing in mind."

If Coble had been at sea, he would have hoisted foul weather flags. It looked like the water was getting rough, wind snapped the sails already.

"Do you suppose I can get a word in here?" He searched his shirt pocket for a peppermint.

Maria ignored him and rejoined the fight. "Don't you have a husband, *Mrs.* Davis?"

Jessica shot a startled glance at her. "My husband is dead."

"Oh. I'm so sorry to hear that." Maria paused a moment. "Arsenic?"

Jessica looked furiously at Maria, her reply cut short by the door banging open again.

Pete stepped quickly into the room and then skidded to a stop as if he had just seen a rattler. "Whoa! What's going on here?"

Coble tried hard not to laugh. It was a losing battle. "I think it's a cat fight. Heard of them, but never saw one. Anyone seen my peppermint?"

Jessica shook her head. "I'm sorry for getting you into this, Coble."

"Sorry?" He stared at her a moment. "Why?"

"You've been here two days and two men are dead. It seems you're living up to the reputation Caleb spoke about."

"You're wrong, lady," Maria said as she struggled against a hasty grab by Coble. "I shot that man in the street, and it was a damned good shot. You might keep that in mind. I take guarding the marshal's back very seriously."

Jessica stiffened, and then a slow smile came to her lips. "Well, now...I'll just bet you do." Her attention turned to Coble. "Mr. Bray, I'll talk to you later about the progress of your investigation. Since you are so...busy, maybe it's a good thing I hired extra help. For now, I'll leave you to your...*ministrations*."

Hearing another growl, he almost didn't catch Maria. He reached out and grabbed her around the waist. Pete hastily backed off as Jessica bustled from the room.

"Pete, did you know your daughter hisses like a cat? It's actually kind of a mixture of hissing and growling. I never heard the like."

She gave him an innocent look. "I don't think your Mrs. Davis likes me."

"You mind your manners, girl." Pete tossed a couple of packages on the bed. "Did she say something about hiring someone to help?"

He immediately sobered. "Yeah, she did. Somehow, she hired Onofrio Perez."

Pete stared at him a moment. "Shit. That ain't good."

Coble continued. "On the advice of Sheriff Stiles."

Pete rolled his eyes.

"Who is this Perez?" Maria asked.

Her father answered, "Bounty hunter...and a stone-cold killer when the price is right." Pete glanced at him and he nodded back. "Or, if there's something to be gained at the end. That woman may not know what she hired."

"I don't think Perez will be a worry now. I set Captain Meyers on his tail."

"Meyers?" Pete gave him a puzzled look.

"I think the good captain has an interest in Jessica."

Maria's frown turned into a smile.

Pete stared at her for a moment, then turned

back to Coble. "So, what's on your mind? We ain't been here long enough to find out much."

"Oh, you'd be surprised. Our brand-new sheriff got drunk and spilled the beans." He spent a few minutes filling them in on everything he'd found out. "All hell is about to break loose around here. There are four girls dead, not two, and we must find some way to put a cork in that particular bottle."

Maria came to sit next to him on the bed, silent tears streaming down her face. The bed sagged so badly it threw them together, shoulder to shoulder. Pete occupied the only chair in the room.

"There is no doubt about this?" Maria's voice was low.

He shrugged. "At least with this, I think the sheriff was honest. I sure as hell wouldn't trust him on anything else."

She sighed as she leaned against him. "Those poor girls."

He looked at his hands a moment, wondering how Pete would feel if he put an arm around her. Just to comfort her of course. "It's a damned shame, but the girls are gone, tragic as it is. Now, I'm not an expert on these things—"

Maria interrupted. "I think we need to concentrate on two things. The families of these girls are mad, which is understandable, but we need to cool them down long enough to let us work. What we don't need is a bloodbath of innocents killed just because they are strangers or strange looking."

He looked at her, then at Pete. "What kind of school did she go to?"

"I'm wondering that myself. It was supposed to be a finishing school."

She elbowed him in his sore ribs. "Also, we need to stop this killing. Fast. Let's not forget that."

He smiled at her. "We won't forget. The problem is, we don't know if the killer is a him, a her, or a combination of both. We've been assuming it's a man, but remember Ma and Pa Bender from over around Independence, Kansas. They killed a lot of people, then disappeared. No one ever found them."

Maria looked at her father and then at him. "What about that? Do you think it could be them?"

"Well, no. I was just using them as an example."

Pete's voice was stern. "There was a reason they disappeared."

Maria wouldn't let it go. "And?"

Coble looked uncomfortably at Pete. When he got a nod, he answered her question. "There was never anything official on their disappearance. They killed the wrong person. That person had friends. The Benders came up missing. End of story." He looked pointedly at her. "Please."

He held her gaze a moment and then turned to the tracker. "We need to move fast. I want you to go talk to Pop Janus."

"Pop's in town? I ain't seen him in a while." Pete brightened.

"The last I saw of him, he'd thrown a saddle on a

wicker chair in front of the boarding house. You go talk to him and see if anyone new has moved into the area. He'll know. Get what information on the people around these hills that you can, then hit the trail."

"All right, I can do that. But once I get saddled and gone, just what do you want me to do?"

"Talk to people. Tell Pop to talk to everyone he knows. Let them know what's going on. We need to be very visible with this. I want the killer to know that everyone's looking for him, and for sure, we think it's a man—we'll go with that for now. Tell people who you work for, don't hide a thing. Most of all, try to find out how many families have young girls and warn them. We need to get the word out to everyone so there's absolutely no opportunity for any more girls to be taken."

"What about me?" Maria asked. "I can help."

He thought a moment while the others stared at him. Finally... "Maria, I want you to stay with me."

"One thing we're not talking about," Pete said. "Any idea who tried to shoot you to rag dolls?"

He smiled grimly. "Oh, I have a very good idea who they are." He told them about what happened at Jessica's house and then the sheriff's office. "Those boys will just have to be put on the back burner for a while. They will be around when I want them."

AFTER PETE LEFT, Maria smiled. "Now, take that shirt off."

"Maria, I don't think right now is the time—"

"You're bleeding all over yourself and ruining that bedspread." She unbuttoned his shirt and then helped him slide it off his shoulders. With light fingers, she traced the raised welts and scars on his chest, then lightly touched the welt on his side. "My god. How many times have you been hurt?"

He looked down at himself. "Just shot, or does cutting count?"

She stood with her hand resting on his chest. "How long can you keep this up? You can't do this forever."

"It does seem like a lot lately. I guess I'll keep going as long as the Lord wants to keep me alive and my luck doesn't run out."

He studied her eyes and the light sprinkling of freckles on her nose and watched a smile start on her lips. She liked being watched.

"Kind of a fatalistic attitude, don't you think? My father told me a lot about you, but never this side. So, this is the way you think? Is that why you're so good at what you do? You just don't care? Everything is out of your hands. Live or die, and the devil take the hindmost? It's all the same to you?"

"Maybe. I think it's a good thing we don't know when we'll cash it in. If we're afraid of dying, then nothing would ever get done."

He tried to stand and winced as the wound started bleeding again.

"Look." It came out harsher than he intended. "When I die, it'll be like pulling your finger out of a pool of water. You'll see a few ripples, then the water smooths out, and the world goes on."

She searched his eyes again a moment. "That is foolish and arrogant."

He responded angrily. "Maybe what you hear is the sound of a man who knows he can be a tool, and also knows he can wear out or be thrown away."

She laughed, and he didn't expect it. "Now you're a pouting, arrogant fatalist? Maybe you just need something to live for. Or someone. And regardless of what you think, you will be missed." When he didn't reply, she continued. "For one thing, you will be missed by your children."

He hadn't known Maria long, but already marveled at her ability to defuse his anger. "Do you think we need to see the local preacher first, before we start on children?"

She was, for once, speechless. At least for about ten seconds. Then she smiled at him. "Well, it's a little quick, and you haven't talked to Pete about it yet, but I think something can be worked out."

He looked at her with his mouth hanging open and then smiled. "Uh, that wasn't a marriage proposal."

She was still grinning at him. "I understand. I am not a young and naïve girl. Sometimes you might want to try something on before you buy it. I feel that way too. It's not a deal breaker. But later, I'll insist on it."

"On what?"

"The preacher, stupid."

"Look, you're a beautiful—"

Maria went up on tiptoes and kissed him on the corner of his mouth. "You're sweet." Her giggling as she went out the door turned to a full peal of laughter after the door closed.

He stood facing the door.

What the hell had just happened?

Chapter Thirteen

WITH MARIA OUT IN THE HALL TALKING WITH her father, Coble went to the packages on the bed. First was a new shirt with wide pockets and a military cut. He grunted with approval at the buckskin, gray color, and soft feel. He'd owe Pete some money for this. In the next package, a new Colt .45 Peacemaker spilled out, along with enough brass shells to start a small war. Hefting the gun, he walked around the room, pointing at several objects, trying to get a feel for the new grip. He took out his old Navy gun and placed it reverently on the stand next to the bed. The .45 Peacemaker was shorter than the Navy gun and didn't fit his holster well, which led to the third package. A new shell belt and holster. Christmas.

Maria walked back in as he was strapping on the new gun belt, standing so close he could have buried his face in her hair.

"You are a very lucky man," she said.

"You're repeating yourself." He resisted an impulse to pull her closer.

"She is very pretty, this Jennifer."

He gave her a wary glance. "Jessica. Her name is Jessica and you damn well know it."

"She is an older woman, with a lot of experience, I think. And a widow with land?"

He gave her a puzzled look. "Not so old. About my age, I'd expect. Where are you going with this?"

She watched him intently. "I think she wants you."

He shook his head. "She just buried her daughter. She isn't looking for a suitor."

Maria laughed softly, her breath a gentle wind on his face. "Men are so stupid. She is a woman. You are a man. But she is dangerous. Did you notice she is not grieving for a lost daughter? She isn't acting right. All I see is anger. A lot of anger."

"People grieve in different ways." He shrugged. "Not everyone is the same."

"I will *not* let her use you. There's something that is not right about her."

"Maybe I don't mind being used." He smiled at her. "Besides, didn't we just have this conversation a few minutes ago? You've got my back...remember?"

"Like I said, you're a man. You have no idea what you need in a woman."

With that statement, she leaned forward and kissed him full on the lips. The kiss lingered a moment. "I am not as young as you think, Coble."

"Maria?" He gently moved away.

She gave him a bright smile. "Yes?"

"I have boots older than you. My saddle could be your grandmother."

"You ride a female saddle?" Her grin was infectious. "That is very interesting. I always thought a saddle looked rather...male."

———

AS THEY MOVED DOWN the hall toward the stairs, there was the sound of running feet. Pete appeared in front of them, too winded from stomping up the stairs to speak.

Finally. "Coble." He held his hands against his side. "Some men have braced Caleb downstairs. There's a bunch of them. It looks like a setup."

While the hotel didn't boast a full saloon, it did have a sitting room with a bar and a few tables. He was at the head of the stairs in a few seconds, Pete and Maria right behind him. As he reached the bottom of the stairs, he saw the room as a mosaic of faces painted in fear and expectation. A few men, the smart ones who'd seen a gunfight before and knew how often bystanders were hit by stray bullets, were quietly slipping away out the side door, while others ringed the outside walls and looked on like bystanders at some natural disaster.

A rough voice filled the void. "Come on, McGill. You don't have a badge for protection anymore. Why don't you reach for that gun and show us how tough you are? I've been waiting for this a long time."

The unshaven man doing the talking was as wide as he was tall. He stood waiting with his hand just above the butt of his holstered pistol. Two men stood off to one side, waiting for the old man to make a move.

Caleb McGill stood next to the bar, and the sight made Coble think of a grizzled old bear facing a pack of timber wolves. The old sheriff might take one or two, but three? It was too many. As he stepped down from the stairs, a slow look of resolve came to the old man's face. Caleb was about to make his try.

"Now don't this beat all?" Coble's voice carried across the room. "It's an old-fashioned gunfight, just like in the dime novels."

In the sudden silence, he distinctly heard the slow double-click of a hammer being drawn back on a revolver. Since the sound came from behind him, and Maria was so close on his heels he could feel her breath, it must be hers.

Where had she hidden a pistol?

"Caleb, you're being selfish. We all know you can kill this ugly cuss with the dirty face and big mouth, but why hog these other two? It's just not fair."

"Mister, you got no business in this," the wide man blustered.

He turned and placed his hand on Maria's chest to stop her at the bottom of the stairs, eliciting a small gasp from her. It was a nice chest. He then gave her a little shove, meaning stay put, and a quick smile just for emphasis, and then replied to the man.

"Oh, I have a big stake in this. Mr. McGill has information I need, and neither of us has time for a would-be bad man with a loud mouth getting in the way of our conversation."

He stood beside the old man, directing his attention on the other two assailants but keeping the wide man in sight. "Caleb, go ahead and kill him. We have work to do and no time to fool around. These two dead men over here won't bother you one bit."

"Pepper?" One of the two men spoke up. "There'll be another day. Let it go."

The man called Pepper was sweating. He hadn't had a bath in a very long time, and the more he sweated the more it became obvious to everyone around him, and also obvious to the whole room his plan had failed. His gaze darted to the other men and then toward the door.

Coble saw the look, recognized the hesitation for what it was, and walked right up to him. "Now, you listen to me. Pepper, is it? You walk out of here. Leave town. Leave the country. If I ever see you again, anywhere, I'll kill you. If you ever see this old man again, you walk to the other side of the street, or better yet, you run the other way. Don't you ever give this man trouble again. If I hear about any trouble, I'll find you and kill you." His voice was very soft. "Do you understand me?"

Pepper didn't make a sound, just stood trying to swallow with a mouth suddenly gone dry.

Coble didn't let up. "If you can't speak, just nod your head, Pepper."

The man nodded.

"Do you know who I am?"

"You're..." After a couple of tries, the man croaked, "You're Coble Bray."

"Do you have any doubt that I'll do what I said?"

Pepper shook his head. "N-no."

He stared at Pepper for a moment. "Excellent. Get out of here, and take those two deadbeats with you."

After watching them leave, he walked to the old sheriff, holding out his hand. "You about through here?"

Shaking his hand firmly, Caleb grinned. "I reckon so."

Coble nodded, still watching the trio of men leave. "Let's all walk over to the sheriff's office. That boy has some explaining to do."

Maria walked up to them, still holding her short-barreled Colt revolver.

"Now where in hell do you keep that?" Coble asked, using that excuse to look at her closely.

She smiled at him. "If you had cooperated just a little more while we were upstairs, you might have found out."

BILLY STILES WASN'T in the office when they arrived, so they grouped around the table.

Coble made eye contact with each of them before he spoke. "I don't think the sheriff will be back. He's probably sleeping off the contents of that empty whiskey bottle he left here. Caleb, we need to know everything you know, and in a hurry."

"It's not much. And it's bad. We got three little girls—"

Maria held up four fingers.

"Four?" Caleb asked in a pained voice.

"Isabel Jakes. We found her last night." Her expression was a mixture of sadness and anger.

"Isabel...?" Caleb slowly rubbed his eyes with his hands. "Pretty little thing. I liked her." He took a big, slow breath and then looked around the table. "That'll change things some. We may have a shooting war on our hands."

"Is that Isaiah Jakes's daughter?" Pete said. "If it is, he lives by the feud. I know him. He could be real trouble."

"So," Caleb said, "we have four girls killed, and I don't have a real clue about any of them. I never found a trail to follow. Nothing. No one saw anything. The girls just vanish, until they show up dead."

Coble started to speak but was interrupted by Maria. "Actually, we do know a few things."

"And just who are you?" Caleb asked her.

"She's my daughter," Pete answered.

Caleb looked stunned. "I didn't know you had any family."

"You and a few others around here," Pete said, glancing at Coble.

"So," she said again, forcefully. "What we do know is this. We're looking for a woodsman. Someone who gets around really good in the forest. Right? A city boy can't disappear like this man has done."

"That really narrows it down, Maria," Coble said.

Maria shot him a scalding look. "We know this person is religious, or at least has a good knowledge of the Bible."

"How do you know that?" Caleb asked. "Besides, most poor people learn to read from the Bible. It's usually the only book they own. That's not odd."

"Well," Maria said, "whoever did this made a cross from vines, then placed it in front of the last girl. That doesn't mean much by itself, but Coble trailed the man from Isabel Jakes's body, and we found a figure of a snake drawn in the dirt, with the words *I AM* written in the dirt under it."

Caleb scratched his head and looked at Pete. "Figure of a snake. Cheyenne?"

Pete just shrugged and shook his head. "Cheyenne wouldn't be quoting the Bible."

No one commented on his sarcasm.

"Anything else, Detective?" Coble asked Maria.

"Yes." She looked him in the eyes. "He doesn't

like girls too much." She paused a moment, think-ing. "Or, maybe he does..."

He looked at her, interested in a woman's point of view for a change. "What are you thinking?"

"I can't put it in words yet. Just something I feel. If all these girls were about the same age, they were about to enter womanhood. Maybe he's trying to save them from that. Maybe he experienced a bad woman in his past."

"You one of those fortune tellers the Gypsies have?" Caleb's voice was sarcastic. "We've all experienced some of that."

Coble's palm slapped down on the table, inter-ceding before Maria could take a chunk out of Caleb. "Okay. All that's right interesting but doesn't get us any closer to the killer. So here's the plan."

"Pete, I want you to go with Caleb. Follow the same plan we talked about earlier and start talking to people. Get as many people as possible to help you and make a lot of noise. Everyone and their off-uncle Fred needs to know about this. The only way to slow this down is to make everyone our eyes and ears. I want to make it too risky for the killer to try and take another girl. We know when the bodies were found, but what we really need to know is when they went missing. This man may be keeping them captive a while. Maybe about a week. If he is, someone has seen or heard something. I'll try to head off this Isaiah Jakes. We have too many deaths around here already."

He thought a moment, holding up his hand

when Pete started to say something. "One more thing. We need a map. These girls were hidden somewhere. If we can get some kind of idea where their bodies were discovered and put it on a map, we might get an idea of the area we're talking about."

"I'll go to the bank," Caleb said. "They hold paper on about every place around. If they don't, they'll still have a record of where the land is because them damned carpetbaggers want all of it."

Pete looked askance at his friend. "What are you going to do? Stay in town and rest?"

"Nope." He grinned at them. "Look, there's not much use combing the countryside looking for a trail or any kind of clue. That's already been done. Even if there was a trail, it would have been ridden over. What I want to do is make the killer uncomfortable. Just like we'd make a lot of noise and drive a mountain lion toward a trap, I want to drive this guy into the open. First, Maria and I are going to church. Maybe the local parson can shed some light on this. Sometimes they see things most people don't."

"And after that?" Maria asked.

"Why," Coble said with a straight face. "I thought we'd go to the local whorehouse."

"I..." Maria's face turned crimson, and then she caught on. "That's a good idea. If anyone would know of any men with, uh"—if possible, she turned even more red—"strange needs, it would be the local girls."

Coble shook his head, marveling at her. As usual, she was way ahead of him.

Pete looked at Caleb. "He's taking my daughter to a whorehouse."

"I heard that," Caleb said. It'll be hard to do, though. We don't have one."

Pete snorted as he choked back a laugh. "None you know of."

"Well, there are a few women, you know...down on their luck..."

"Uh-huh."

Chapter Fourteen

THE TWO MEN PICKED UP THEIR OLD FRIENDSHIP as if they'd been apart only a few days instead of years, already arguing about everything and nothing in particular.

After they left, Maria got up and closed the door. "We need to talk."

Coble settled back into his chair, watching closely as she moved toward him. "You're going to tell me you like to dress like a man."

She gasped and looked like she was about to take flight. "How'd you know?"

"It took me a while." He grinned. "Something bothered me about you all along. I just couldn't put my finger on it."

She walked around the table. "Was it my hands? I knew I'd made a mistake with my hands."

"Nope. Two things. Your eyes. Your walk."

"You watched me walk?" Her smile grew as she watched him.

It was his turn to be defensive. "Well, you were posing as a man. But you didn't exactly walk like a man. Men walk...different."

Edging up to him, her fingers moved idly over his chest. "You like to watch men walk? Do you like girly boys, Mr. Bray? Have I lost already?"

He held his fingers to his temples and rubbed. Big headache coming on. "Was there something else you wanted to talk about? Other than you dressing as a boy?"

She took a deep breath and seemed to be debating with herself. Finally... "I have a small confession to make. Instead of going to school, I got a job as a Pinkerton agent. Have been for several years. Back east." Seeing his expression, she backed a step and stammered, "Well, several places."

He sat up straight, stunned.

She continued. "I was, I *am* on assignment."

"God in heaven. What kind of assignment?"

Her legs weakened and she collapsed in a chair. She seemed to be debating with herself. "The agency knew I was coming out to meet my father, so what I'm supposed to do is send back names and descriptions of potential outlaws, bank robbers, and the like, along with where to find them."

"Outlaws...bank robbers...and the like...where to find them." He repeated her words in a daze and then suddenly became quiet, his heart thudding slowly in his chest. "How are you supposed to send this information? And this is damned important."

She wouldn't meet his gaze while she nervously

fiddled with a short stack of papers on the table. "I am supposed to send a telegram to the office in Kansas City."

"Christ." His breath escaped in a long sigh as he tried to count nails in the ceiling above. "You're either an idiot or a fool. Maybe both."

"Coble, I—"

He pinned her with his gaze. "Shut up and listen to me. Have you sent any messages? Anything at all?"

"No." Her voice was tremulous. "Not yet."

"Thank God. How are you keeping information? In your head? How?"

She reached into a pocket and pulled out a tally book. "Here. With this."

He snatched it from her and took it to the stove. He pulled a match from his pocket and lit the book on fire.

"Hey!" She lunged at him.

He tossed the flaming book into the stove, slammed the door, and opened the damper so the blaze wouldn't go out. Turning, he put his hands on her shoulders.

"Listen to me, Maria. Your life depends on this. Mine does too because I'll try to protect you if anything happens. Anyone can read a telegram. People talk. There are no secrets in this country. Don't you ever breathe another word about your job to anyone. Don't ever say the word Pinkerton or agent. As of this moment, you have never heard of either of those words. If this ever gets out, you're dead. Do you understand me? Dead."

He stared at her defiant eyes a moment. He wasn't getting through to her. "Have you heard of John Whicher?"

"No, I haven't."

"Damned right you haven't. I'll bet they never mentioned that around your office. He's dead. He was a Pinkerton agent sent here to look around. How about Dan Askew or Jack Ladd?"

"No. Neither." Her voice wavered.

"Funny your boss didn't mention them to you. They're all dead. They were Pinkerton agents sent into this country just to look around."

She cleared her throat a couple of times. "I gather Pinkerton agents aren't well-liked around here."

"With damned good reason." He released his grip on her shoulders. "This isn't funny. The people around here aren't as bad as they're made out to be back east in the papers."

Maria's voice regained strength. "If they rob banks and kill people, they should be in jail or hung. It's the law."

"Even if a federal judge turned the deeds to their homes over to a bank, and then that bank makes them buy their own land back while using the Army to back up their swindles? Where does a backcountry, hardscrabble farmer get that kind of money?"

"You condone what they do? Robbing and killing?"

"No, I don't agree with what goes on. But I do understand why it happens. I understand why they're forced to do what they do. And to them, they are being forced. Most of the people making the trouble could just move on, and a lot have. But there's a lot of pride involved here. This is their land —and their father's and grandfather's land before them. They will stand their ground."

He met her gaze in a match of wills. "Don't do it, Maria." His voice was pleading. "If you don't believe me, talk to Pete. Talk to Caleb. Hold your judgment until you know the people. Concentrate on what's going on around here right now. Help me."

Her voice was soft. "I didn't think you needed much help."

He looked at her a moment and then shrugged. "Good Lord, Maria. Can't you see I'm out of my element here? You've already thought of things I'd never have thought of. It's the same for Pete and Caleb. This is new ground for us, and it's a whole hell of a lot worse crime than robbing banks."

Impulsively, he reached out and took her hand. "The West is a pretty small community. Generally, we know about where people are located and what they're doing. With the railroad and telegraph, communication between lawmen about known criminals is getting a lot easier. My job's simple. If I go after someone, I usually know where to look for them. Sometimes I already know them. If they start running, they leave a trail I can follow. If I put the word out that I'm looking for someone, and they pop up in a town where the sheriff knows this, I get a telegram. The real bad ones always think they're better and smarter than anyone else, so sometimes they just wait for me and fight it out."

He paused and let out a deep breath.

"Whatever is going on here is different. There's no trail here, and damn few clues. All we have are bodies. Caleb, the Army, and just about everyone else has been up and down every trail around here and found nothing. And I gotta believe the locals know the country better than any of us." He was lost in thought a moment, and that thought was haunting him. "I have a gut feeling the killer may be walking by us on the street. We just can't see him."

She released his hand and stood. "Then I'll go and talk to people around town. That's what I'm good at. Maybe you can help out more than you think by hitting the trails along with the other men."

"No, not yet. Caleb and Pete can take care of that. The more I think about it, I don't think we'll find this guy out in the woods. And, no more talk of the Pinks or sending them information. Promise me?"

"I promise."

"All right." His sigh was relieved this time. "Jessica is supposed to be bringing this parson around so we can talk. I'll wait for them at the church. You can nose around and talk to people. Let people know right up front that you're helping Pete, Caleb, and me. And be careful. Later, I'll go to the saloon and talk to a few of the girls. Now that I think of it, I guess this town is too small for a crib house."

She chuckled at him. "You sound disappointed about the crib."

"What do you know about cribs?"

"Hey." She laughed. "I'm the one from the big city."

"It's still not something nice girls should know about."

She gave him a serious look. "And just what is it that nice girls should know about? Knitting and sewing? Cooking and having babies?" She paused, shaking her head. "I know you are older than me, both in years and experience. But I'd like my chance to help."

He didn't say anything.

"Besides, you lied to me."

"What?" His eyebrows shot up.

"Your boots look new."

Chapter Fifteen

COBLE DIDN'T MAKE IT TO THE CHURCH. LEAVING the sheriff's office, he met Jessica walking down the boardwalk.

After the rains the day before, the air was clear and warm, with a promise of summer on the way. Taking a big breath, he savored the moment, knowing the weather didn't give a damn and that the peace and quiet was a sham.

"You mentioned a preacher. How often does he come around?"

She shrugged, looking away from him. "Once every month or so. He's not real regular. We can kind of schedule the weddings and christenings. Funerals...we're usually on our own for that."

He thought about that for a moment. "Seems odd to me. Him not doing funerals, I mean."

"Why?"

"I'm just thinking out loud. Weddings and christenings are events that bring in a lot of young people. Especially young girls. It's more social. But funerals? That's where the minister gets a chance to preach about repentance and salvation—hellfire and brimstone, so to speak. Unless there's a reason he doesn't like funerals."

She stared at him a moment, then shook her head as if to clear it. "You know, it was so easy to get a preconceived idea of what you're like after hearing about you from Caleb. He talked of you so often I thought I knew you. Now I need to start over. I just realized I don't know you at all. Especially where your head goes at a time like this. Are you spooky smart, or do you just throw a lot of mud at the wall to see what sticks?"

He gave her a rueful grin. "I once heard an old German say, 'Too soon old, too late smart.' I'm afraid that applies to me."

"Well, your idea that a preacher could be a killer is preposterous. Surely a man of the cloth couldn't be on your list of suspects?"

He almost laughed aloud, thinking of Priest. "You've led a very sheltered life. Right now, everyone's on the list except the mothers of the children. For a mother to kill a child would be a very rare occurrence."

"I'll have you know I'm very well read. I've actually been educated well beyond the fourth grade."

People passed them by occasionally and she nodded to them with a smile. A couple of younger women walked by and she put her hand on his arm —a bit of a possessive show. Funny, but he didn't mind until he thought of her and a certain captain. He slid her hand off his arm. The more he thought about it, his choices from that line of thinking would either get his eyes scratched out, or just shot dead. Thinking of how Maria had backed him up when they'd come to Caleb's aid, he took an extra step away from her.

She noticed and arched an eyebrow. "I need to purchase a few things. You'll be all right? Not get lost?"

He thought a moment of the one-street town, compared to Kansas City. "I'll make out."

A voice interrupted them. "Well, you two make a fine-looking couple."

He turned to find the judge and another man standing on the boardwalk in front of them.

"Marshal Bray, I thought you were leaving town and here I find you strolling the boardwalk with a beautiful woman."

"I never said I'd leave, Judge. You should remember that I don't like to leave a job unfinished. All the pins holding your carefully crafted scenario together have come out. All I find are lies."

While speaking, he barely glanced at the judge. All his attention was on the man standing to the side. Medium-sized and nattily dressed. Not a hair out of place under a black bowler hat. Pencil-thin mustache over a weak mouth and chin and the coldest set of eyes he'd ever seen. Not just cold... lifeless. If he'd come face to face with a puma out in the woods, he wouldn't have been more alert. Alarm bells pealed in his head. His bag of snakes analogy came back to him, because here was a rattler. As he continued to stare at the man, startled recognition came into the man's eyes. Recognition that he was being accessed and judged.

The last set of eyes like that he'd seen were attached to a bounty hunter and sure-thing killer who'd made a lot of money in a few range wars. He'd killed people with the same emotion he'd use to step on a bug.

"Who's your friend, Judge?" He didn't break eye contact with the man in question.

Jessica interrupted. "Coble, please don't be rude. This is the circuit rider I told you about and my good friend, Reverend Stone. He's been a real comfort to me these past few weeks."

She turned her attention back to the two men. "I didn't realize you were back, Reverend."

"Just changed my route a little, my dear." The man extended his hand with a mocking smile. "Finias Stone, at your service."

Coble took the limp hand a moment and then dropped it. A limp handshake was a poor judge of a man, but this was like he'd just been handed a dead fish. "What's your particular brand of religion, Reverend? Methodist? Presbyterian? Lutheran? Catholic?"

Reverend Stone shook his head. "None of those. They are much too formal. I just preach the Bible."

"Handy." Coble never wanted to grab his gun so much in his life.

"I beg your pardon?" The lifeless eyes measured him.

"You don't really have to answer to anyone, do you? No one keeps track of you? There is no one to know where you're supposed to be and when you're supposed to be there. No organization or body of peers, nobody looking over your shoulder? No schedule. Like I said. Handy."

Where the judge was nearly apoplectic, showing his anger, the reverend just presented a lifeless smile and dead eyes. How do you show anger with dead eyes?

The man spoke softly. "I answer to God, no other. Maybe you should come to church Sunday. You can judge my brand, as you put it."

Coble let his glance slide from the reverend to the judge. "I might just do that, because I'll definitely be around. You should probably expect me at many of the same places you frequent. Will your sermon be about the slaughter of innocents that's been going on? I was waiting to talk to you anyway. What are your thoughts on the killings? Now that we know the Indian that was murdered by the sheriff was innocent and that none of the girls were scalped. I thought in your line of work you might have seen or heard something that might give us some help. Maybe such a depraved and cowardly individual might have felt remorse and confided or confessed to you? Seeking forgiveness?"

The man turned his full attention on Coble. "It wouldn't matter if I had. Anything like that would be confidential between the parishioner and me. You understand that would be betraying a confidence, don't you?"

"You hold yourself in very high esteem, Reverend. Even your thoughts are privileged? My thinking was that you'd be interested in catching this skunk. I mean"—he stared intently at the man —"this guy is a sick freak, don't you think? Killing little defenseless girls? How low can you be?"

The preacher shrugged. "Sometimes things are not as they seem. Sometimes there are reasons and subtleties a common man like you cannot imagine."

He stared at the man, trying to make the preacher lose his calm demeanor. And he'd leaned a little too hard on the word common. "True. I am common. But, more often than not, things are exactly as they seem. As an educated man, are you familiar with Occam's Razor? A layman's definition would be that the simplest answer is most often true."

Coble shook his head, still watching the man. "One of the advantages of being a *common* man, as you put it, is that I won't be sidetracked by a lot of meaningless dead ends. Once I see the quarry, I keep my eyes on it."

The judge tried to wedge himself between the two men. "Marshal, I really do not see the point to all of this."

"Well, it's simple. I'm just trying to get his professional opinion. It appears he's failing in that regard and doesn't seem to be professional at all."

He turned back to Reverend Stone. "Since you're such a vital part of this community, perhaps I should put someone with you for protection? A traveling companion?"

The man flinched. Got him. Coble smiled.

"No. That will not be necessary." Reverend Stone seemed to recover. "Besides, no one's harming adults. Why would I need protection?"

"Right. Just innocent little girls. Helpless."

"Innocent?" The reverend was again calm and collected as he smiled at Coble. "No one is innocent. We're all born in sin."

"Yeah, that's true," Coble replied. "But God is the arbiter on that, don't you think?"

Jessica gasped, gave Coble an exasperated glance, and then hooked arms with both the judge and reverend. "Mr. Bray, your attitude is appalling. I know these two men and they're above reproach. I'll have these two gentlemen see me to the hotel."

As they walked away, he called out. "Judge, I'll be arresting Sheriff Stiles for murder. It'll be interesting to see who ordered him to do that."

There was no reply.

———

COBLE WAS LEFT to his own devices, and a short walk took him to the church at the end of the street. The winding path was made of flat stone, with steps put in where needed. The grass on both sides was cut down and taken away. The buckboards and buggies would be parked below, he guessed. Kind of inconvenient. Especially in the rain. It looked more showpiece than a working church.

When he walked across the solid porch and tried the door, he was surprised to find it open. A quick glance inside showed a chapel not unlike the one in Kansas City that Priest presided over, and it proved to be empty.

He stood a few moments before the cross, trying to clear his mind. It wouldn't come, and there was no peace here. After a few minutes at the altar, which was little more than a wooden cross nailed to the end wall of the building, he turned away and pulled the door closed. He sat on the front steps, leaning against the porch post, and closed his eyes. He needed to send a telegram to Priest. And he definitely needed to go to church on Sunday, if for no other reason than to irritate Reverend Stone.

For the first time in a long while, he was unsure about how to proceed. In his mind, he was convinced the preacher was the killer. He didn't know why he was so sure, maybe the man just acted too guilty—or too cold. The conviction of the man's guilt was a cold, spidery feeling in his spine. But without catching him actually killing someone, he couldn't think of how to get a conviction.

His instinct was to take him out like a rabid dog and shoot him. But he couldn't, and after their exchange on the boardwalk, he was sure the reverend wouldn't be baited into doing something foolish. What now? For once, he was unsure how to proceed.

————

WHEN HE OPENED HIS EYES, the sun was high and Maria was moving up the walk.

She carried a couple of parcels wrapped in brown paper and tied with white cotton string. Placing the packages next to her, she sat by him. He knew it was coming, so he just waited her out.

Finally, she took a deep breath. "I'm trying hard to understand you."

"I don't envy you." He looked at her with a small grin. "That might be a lifetime endeavor."

"I saw you walking with that Jezebel woman. She was holding your arm, and you looked happy. Do you want her?"

As an investigator, he found himself wondering where she hid her gun. "Her name's Jessica."

She colored slightly but continued. "When we're together, I feel there's an attraction. A connection between us. Can you deny that?"

Warily, he replied. "I wouldn't try to deny it. I'm a man. You're a beautiful woman."

Her gaze never wavered from his, seemed to move closer. "Beyond that."

He watched her a moment and wondered if inquisition was in Spanish blood or just in females in general. Somehow he got lost in her eyes until he shook himself.

"To be honest," he said. "I wouldn't object to exploring that attraction. But you need to understand the difference in us. While you've been shopping, I've been contemplating how to kill a man without any physical proof of wrongdoing."

He continued. "I'm not some knight in shining armor. I'm no hero. I'm just a man who's good with a gun and who has a little judgment. I've killed men. A lot of men. That takes its toll. A man in my business doesn't make long-term plans."

She sighed. "I may have come across a little forward today. I'm sorry. I'm not a loose woman. I just see something I want and reach out to take it. It's the way I am."

As if making her point, she picked up his hand, rubbing the top of it with her own. "Could you give it up? The job, I mean?"

He looked at her with surprise. "I was just inside this sanctuary, trying to figure that out. Somehow I feel The Man isn't too happy with me." With a smile, he continued. "Are we holding hands?"

She dropped his hand, but not before giving it an extra squeeze. "You are a vexing person. And don't dodge the question. Evasion does not suit you."

"Vexing? What kind of word is that?" Her left eyebrow slowly arched. How do women do that? "No one has ever asked me to stop doing what I do. Mostly, they want me to keep going. But for the right reasons..." He paused a moment. "Yes, I can be domesticated."

Her voice was soft. "Would a loving woman and babies be a good enough reason?"

He was starting to sweat. "Again, yes."

"Would you put up your guns? A woman wants to know her man is coming home every day."

He hesitated, although it was an easy question that he'd spent a lot of time thinking about. "No. Of course I wouldn't. You cannot ask me to be something I'm not. A gun is a tool. I think that I can change jobs. I've always wanted a small ranch. Just some horses and a few head of cattle. Peace and quiet. Actually, I've already picked out a place. But I will not give up my guns until they do."

She looked at him with a puzzled frown. "They?"

"The other side. The lawless and people who take advantage just because they're stronger than others. We cannot give the world to them."

They sat shoulder to shoulder, enjoying the day and the cool breeze cutting across the valley. He thought they were comfortable together and liked that they could sit in silence and enjoy each other.

Maria finally broke the silence. "I was inside the store and heard you talking to the minister. You were not very polite."

"If you were in the store, you saw Jessica leaving on the arms of two other men, so that should have answered one question for you." He chuckled and looked at her. "Sometimes the way I get a job done is to let people know I'm here and that I'm looking for the killer. Occasionally, in their arrogance, the killer will find me. I think this one's so full of himself, so sure of his invincibility, that he just cannot stand me not knowing who he is."

"So is that what you're doing? Just waiting around for the killer to find you? That could be dangerous and it could take forever."

"Nope, not forever. It took just a few hours."

She gasped and clutched his arm. "What? You think...?"

He thought of those cold, lifeless eyes. "He's already found me."

———

COBLE ABRUPTLY STOOD in front of Maria, shielding her. A man was riding up the path toward them. He wore a mix and match of homespun trousers and buckskin shirt. A floppy hat sporting several holes was clamped on his head. Coble felt slighted. His hat only had one hole in it.

At a time when most men carried lever action rifles, this man carried an old Sharps .50-caliber buffalo rifle. That gun would shoot clear through a building and the bullet would still be going into next week. While the man looked like he'd not seen the bottom of a bathtub in a long time, the Sharps looked well-oiled, polished, and taken care of.

She stood behind him, gave a little gasp, then stepped around in front. "Hello." She raised her hand in greeting, and the man reined in his horse. "You must be Isaiah Jakes."

The rider gave her a curious glance. "And jest how would you be knowing that?"

"You were pointed out to me when I was in town. I was looking for information on the parents of the girls that were killed. My name is Maria Santos."

"Lot of Santos around." The man measured them both with cold eyes. "Kin to Pete?"

"Daughter," Maria said, nodding.

He raised his left hand to tip his hat. "Nice to meet you, Miz Santos. But pretty as you are, you won't keep me from doing what I came to do."

Coble took note that Isaiah's right hand didn't leave the Sharps.

"I come to talk to this..." Isaiah paused like something unpleasant was in his mouth. "...federal marshal, if he'll just step out from behind your skirts."

Well now. It wasn't a time for the timid. Not with this man. "Mr. Jakes, I'm sorry for your loss. I truly am. I cannot imagine what you must feel. But you'll keep a civil tongue in your head in front of the lady, or I'll pull you off that horse and teach you some manners."

Jakes tightened his grip on the Sharps, eyes narrowing.

"I know you're hurting and want answers." Coble continued. "You want revenge. Someone must pay. I agree with that. But what you're thinking of doing is a really bad idea. How many children do you have?"

"I used to have seven. Now I got six."

He watched Isaiah fight his anger. "It would be a shame to make them orphans. I've heard you're a good man. I don't want to harm you. But I can't take a chance of you firing at me and hitting Maria. I don't want to, but I'll put you down. If you don't believe anything else, believe that."

Jakes's close-set eyes gazed at him over a hawk-billed nose. "I might not be so easy to take, lawman."

Coble sighed. This wasn't going well so he took a chance. "Do you believe in God?"

The man stared at him a moment, and then nodded. "I do. Be a sin to deny that."

"Then hear me out. We're standing in front of a church. As God is my witness, before you can lift that Sharps, or get to the hideout gun hanging under your shirt, you'll be gone. I don't want that to happen. Everything you've heard about me is true. I am that fast."

"Look," he continued. "I know the pain is terrible. So is the anger. Maybe that's what you want? Do you want me to end it for you? Is that what this is all about?"

Maria had been ignored long enough. She stepped wide of the two men. "Speak your piece, Isaiah. I know you are angry and hurt, but Marshal Bray is *not* the enemy here. He is here to help. After all, we've only been here two days."

Isaiah was a proud man. Coble didn't know him personally, but most of these hardscrabble farmers were. They worked from sunup to sundown, never asking for anything from anyone.

Isaiah slowly relaxed and nodded at them. "All right."

Stepping forward, Coble offered his hand. Isaiah's gaze flicked toward the hand, noticing it was his right hand. His gun hand. That seemed to make up his mind. Isaiah nodded again and stepped down from his horse.

Coble glanced at Maria. "Let's have that talk, Isaiah."

———

AN HOUR LATER, Coble and Maria walked him to his horse.

Maria asked, "When will the service for Isabel be?"

Jakes shrugged. "Already done it. As soon as we got her home, we put her in our cemetery with the newborns that didn't make it. She'll rest peaceful there and keep them company until we join them."

Coble was curious. "Why didn't you wait for the preacher?"

"Don't like him." Jakes snorted. "He came around, once. Wanted to lay hands on the old woman and the kids. Said they needed healing. Last I saw of him, he was hightailing it up the trail and was purty far ahead of his horse. He ain't been back."

Jakes looked at them. "Y'all come visit. Anytime.

You make a good couple." He looked at Coble. "And you find that killer."

"I shall. Isaiah, I'd count it as neighborly if you let people know we're here. Watch the trails and keep the kids close. We just need a little time."

As the man rode away, Coble asked, "Maria, I wonder just how many places that preacher visited?"

She picked up her packages, and they started back down the path toward town. He was surprised that it was so late in the day.

He continued. "Since everyone seems to think we're a couple, how about I buy you supper?"

"Are you asking me out?" Brown eyes snapping, she smiled at him.

"Well, even beautiful girls have to eat."

"I bought a new dress, but it's for the wedding. I'll just have to go as I am."

"That's fine." And then her words caught up with him. "Wedding? What wedding? You bought a wedding dress?"

She smiled that bright-as-the-sun smile at him before she turned and walked toward town. "You are not much of a sweet talker, are you?"

Well, hell. He'd lost that race before his horse was out of the starting blocks. Speechless, he watched her a moment as she walked away. It was a nice walk.

He called after her. "Let me run by my room first. I'll meet you in a few minutes."

She just wiggled her fingers at him over her shoulder. "Don't be long."

COMING from a different direction to the hotel, it was easier to enter from the side door. He quietly navigated the stairs to the second floor. Moving toward his room, he noticed Jessica's door was open just a crack and heard voices inside. The voices were muffled, but one sounded like a man. Remembering what she'd said about propriety and not wanting people to know she was in his room, he stopped and peeked in the door, wondering who she was entertaining. The tableau playing out was like a bad dream, or something read in a barber shop paper, or perhaps one of those new dime novels. In the foreground was the reverend, and he was kissing Jessica. While she wasn't fighting it, he wasn't sure if she liked it.

The judge stood behind her, unbuttoning his shirt. Jessica had her hand against the reverend's shoulder, moaning and pushing. Thinking she wasn't a willing partner in this, he had his hand on the knob and started to open the door to stop them when the judge's chuckle stopped his advance into the room. "It sure doesn't take her long to surrender, does it, Finias?"

Jessica's arms slowly lowered limply to her sides as the judge supported her closely from behind. Her handbag fell from her fingers and lightly hit the floor as she started to return his kisses. Hands were roving freely over her body from both men. Her moaning was loud enough to be heard in the hall.

Well now. Coble shook his head. *That* was a new wrinkle.

He backed quietly from the door. Things were falling into place—maybe why the judge was here, and maybe why the judge defended Reverend Stone so vehemently. And why there was no real investigation into the murders? Were they two peas in a pod? Or three? A lot of questions were answered in one little scene, but more followed. He went quietly on to his room to change his shirt.

Chapter Sixteen

THE RESTAURANT CONNECTING TO THE HOTEL wasn't as busy as the night before. Maria and Coble immediately found a table and placed their orders. The girl waiting on them said they didn't need a menu. All they had was beef and potatoes, with all the gravy they wanted.

After the waitress left, Maria commented, "I could do better over a campfire. At least I could fry up some bread, add some peppers and whatnot to the potatoes to spice things up a little."

His mind on the scene he'd left at the hotel, he kept his head down, eating his steak.

She continued. "You might think of that. All the lonely trails, the campfires at night. I could be very useful to have around."

He raised his head and gave her a blank look.

"Of course," she rattled on. "I'd have to give up a lot, too. Being an investigator has been fun, most times."

He snapped his gaze up. "I told you not to talk about that here."

"Look, Coble. I'm a grown woman. I decide what I'm going to talk about."

When he didn't rise to the bait, she asked quietly, "What's wrong? Your body is here, but your head is somewhere else. It's not the proper action for a man asking a woman out to dinner."

He looked at her a moment, then told her what he'd seen in Jessica's room. Almost as shocking as what he'd seen was her lack of condemnation. "She's a grown woman, Coble. Women have needs the same as men. And behind closed doors, who knows. You would do well to remember that."

His reply was cut short when a man stuck his head in the door of the restaurant. "Marshal, you better come quick."

He ran out onto the boardwalk with Maria right behind him.

A small cavalcade rode slowly down the street. An Indian was in front, leading a horse with a body tied over the saddle. Another Indian rode beside a wounded man, helping support him in the saddle. The sun was almost down and the shadows were long. The group rode from deep shadow to sunlight and then back into shadow as the dying daylight streamed between the buildings.

Strangely, he thought of the inane little things that assailed the senses at a time like this. The cadence of the horses as they clip-clopped toward him. The little puffs of dust from their hoof-falls as they neared. Even in the cooling breeze of the evening, he felt a trickle of sweat on his face. From long habit, he started to take off his hat to wipe his brow and realized the hat was on the table inside.

Little things.

The first Indian rode a piebald mustang, the second a roan. Both horses were fine animals and he wondered where they'd acquired them, and how.

He felt Maria's hand on the small of his back and smelled the lilac-scented soap she'd bathed with that day. He heard her breath catch in her throat. Reality flooded back when people erupted out of the buildings to surround the men as they rode up and stopped in front of Coble and Maria.

"Pete!" Maria screamed as she leaped from the walk and ran to the wounded man. With the help of several men, she had him off the horse and they carried him into the hotel. There were calls for the doctor. As they went in, she glanced back with tears in her eyes. She shook her head, fear a mask across her face. He nodded to her. She would expect him to come inside soon.

He already knew the worst. He'd recognized Caleb's horse as they came down the street, and his mind had already accepted the fact that his old friend was dead. How many warriors had come home this way? Caleb had expected it. Maybe it would be Coble's destiny too. He walked out and put his hand on the body, sorrow a deep pit in his stomach. Memories flooded his mind. He remembered something Caleb had told him once when he'd asked the old man if he was afraid of dying.

"King Henry said it best at the Battle of Agincourt. The battle is before us and we cannot change it or make it go away. And an old man is a pitiful thing."

Looked like he'd gotten his wish.

Pop appeared suddenly with a couple of men. "We'll take him." His voice was soft. When Coble didn't respond, it grew louder. "C'mon, son. Let us take care of him. Let us have him."

He finally stepped back and let Caleb's friends take over, watching them until, as gently as they could, they loaded him onto a door and took his body into the livery. Finally, he looked up at the lead Indian who waited patiently.

"Wild Pony," Coble said. "It's been a long time."

The man nodded. "Much time has passed."

The growing crowd pressed in and he whirled on them. "You folks go on about your business. You'll find out what's going on soon enough."

He stared them down, and finally, most of the crowd edged away. He turned back to Wild Pony. "Talk to me. Tell me what happened."

The man shrugged. "We heard gunfire. One volley. You know what that means. It sounded like an ambush, so we went to look. We found McGill and the other man we do not know. Their horses were standing with them along the trail. We heard other horses riding away, but it was starting to get dark and we did not follow. The one man needed your medicine man. We brought the men here."

Coble nodded as he looked up at Wild Pony. "You did the right thing. Thank you."

Most people would have been surprised at how well Wild Pony spoke English, but Coble wasn't. Wild Pony was as wild as his name implied, but he was better educated than the average settler. The man had attended different mission schools on reservations, but starvation and idiot Indian agents had driven him away. He was an older man, and his passion ran deep.

Coble was puzzled and took a deep breath. "Why are you here? You're a long way from Oklahoma."

"There is a woman of the Otoe. My son heard of her beauty and came to see her. We came with him and brought many horses. My woman needs grand-children before she is too old to spoil them. My son was killed." Wild Pony hesitated a moment. "He was my only son."

"Was he killed by the Otoe?"

"No. We have come for the man who did it, but he is always surrounded by many men. We wait. Our time will come."

He thought of the Indian scalp Billy Stiles had shown him. All the pieces of the puzzle were fitting together. "I'm sorry. I've heard of this. That man will pay. You have my word on it."

"White man's justice takes a long time." Wild Pony smiled grimly. "Sometimes it does not work at all."

A germ of an idea formed. There'd be little

cooperation from the judge about any of this. Also, the judge was squarely behind Sheriff Stiles and maybe pulling his strings.

"Perhaps we can help each other." He described Reverend Stone. "If this man rides out of town, I want to know every place he goes. It's my belief this man is the one killing young girls, but I may not be able to prove it for our court of law."

Wild Pony thought about it. "I have heard of these killings. We will watch. You take care of the killer of my son. Just don't wait too long." He looked directly at Coble. "I have enough men to come into town and get him. We would lose many, but it would be a warrior's death."

"I understand. It would be a bad thing if you did this. Give me a little time." Wild Pony gave a curt nod.

"One other thing. If you see us have a town meeting or a trial, keep a close watch. If you see Sheriff Stiles and the Reverend Stone ride out of town together, it will mean I've failed to bring them to justice. Then they're all yours. Do you understand?"

A ghost of a smile crossed Wild Pony's face as he nodded. "We will watch."

"I appreciate it," Coble said. "Do you need anything? Grub? Tobacco?"

"We have what we need." With that, the two Indians wheeled their horses and rode between buildings and out of town.

Before he could move, another man stepped off

the boardwalk to stand beside him. Surprised, Coble said, "Hello, Frank. Seems like forever since I saw you in Kansas City. Have I got any money left there?"

Frank snorted. "I'd be more worried about the banker than me. I want you to know this deal with Caleb wasn't any of ours. None of our kin or friends would have anything to do with this. Caleb was a good man. He had our respect. There were times when he chased us all over hell and gone, and we've traded shots a time or two. But we would never back-shoot him."

Coble nodded. "I know that, and I have my suspicions. But if you want to help, I need names, Frank. Soon."

Frank nodded. "How about right now? That's one of the reasons I came to see you. Texas Johnny Cade and Chico Cruz. There were some others, but I don't know them."

"Are you sure?"

Frank shrugged as he answered with a grim expression. "You have my word on it, for what it's worth."

"Your word has always been good enough for me." He thought for a moment. Both men had endured their share of battles, and not always on the same side of the law. They weren't friends, more like adversaries who fully understood each other.

Finally..."Stay clear of this, Frank. And keep your people clear. I'll handle it."

"Those two knuckleheads can throw some lead. If you need help?"

Coble shook his head. "Well, you know what they say? Life's a bitch, then you die. I'm going to take the gloves off. But I'll read to them from the Book first...and if I cash it in here, I won't go alone."

"There's one other small item. I kinda hate to bring it up. Seems like the Pinks are getting cute again. Word is they've sent a woman to do their dirty work this time. I have a name about who it is, but you won't like it. If you're sweet on that girl of Pete's, you'd better set her straight. Some of our people aren't just real particular when it comes to Pinkertons."

Coble shook his head, cursing softly. He was afraid it would come to this. "All right, here's what I know." He went on to tell Frank about Maria and how her boss had enlisted her. "I've talked to her. I've also retired her. She hasn't sent any information, which I'm sure you already know. And she will not. She's good people."

Frank grinned. "Yeah, I thought so. You *are* sweet on her. I'll put the word out not to bother her."

He put his hand on Frank's shoulder. "Do more than that. It would be war. I know she got off on the wrong foot around here, but if anything happens to her, you'd better kill Pete and me, and everyone we know between here and Texas."

He was still grinning, but the humor had left

Frank's eyes. "Well, now. I guess that's plain enough."

As Coble turned to walk back into the building to check on Pete, he saw Reverend Stone on the boardwalk, smiling his little smile. Already mad, he detoured toward Stone and spoke quietly, staring into those dead eyes.

"It's coming on dark, Reverend. You could catch your death from the chill."

"I rather like the night," said Stone. "It's very soothing to me."

"Get used to it. There's a very special place for animals like you. Soon, that darkness is all you'll see."

He looked around to make sure no one could hear before he spoke. "You can't prove anything against me. Your impotence is amusing. Now, go away from me and tend to your harlot."

People were starting to crowd the boardwalk, so he didn't react. He stared at Stone a moment. "Your day will come."

———

COBLE WALKED INTO THE HOTEL. He had to let Jessica know about Caleb and check on Pete. He received a nod and point from the man behind the counter and took the stairs two at a time. A knot of men clustered around the first room he came upon, so he simply entered.

Pete was flat on his back on the bed and Maria

held a compress on his shoulder. She was a vision of beauty, black hair shining in the lamp glow, with blood staining her hands and wrists as she assisted the doctor. When she glanced at him, her eyes were big and tears ran down her cheeks, but she was doing what needed to be done. There was iron in this girl.

A man he assumed was a doctor raised from the side of the bed, holding a slug in a pair of forceps. "Got it!"

Hearing a door close, Coble stepped back into the hall as Jessica came from her room.

At his expression, she asked, "What's happened?"

"It's bad news. Caleb and Pete were ambushed. Pete is being worked on by the doctor." He stopped a moment and cleared his throat.

She leaned against the wall with her hand covering her mouth.

"Caleb's dead, Jessica. I'm sorry. I know you were close."

She flinched and stepped back. Visibly gathering herself, she touched his arm. "As were you. I'm sorry. He always spoke so highly of you."

Her grip tightened on his arm as she tried to pull him closer. When he resisted, she stopped. "Coble, what...?"

"I saw you in the room with your lovers," he said. "You're riding a hard trail."

She gasped, then turned red before giving him a

sad look. "So, I'm not the chaste widow you thought I'd be?"

"Nothing like that at all. Your life's your own. You told me that once, and I respect it."

Her eyes were shiny with unshed tears and she slumped against the wall again. Then she straightened, chin up. "I'm not a whore."

"I didn't say you were. But then, I'm not a voyeur, so I didn't stay around long enough to see if any money changed hands."

The slap turned his head to the side. Then she held a hand to her mouth. "Damn you. I just...get lonely. I'm not any less of a person for that."

"And that man I killed on your doorstep, had he been there before?" She lowered her head and couldn't meet his gaze.

"Yes."

"Well, most people say that I'm just a killer with a badge. Sometimes I think they're right. Who am I to judge? I'd better check on Pete. Next time, make sure your door's closed."

———

COBLE MOVED BACK to the room. He was sad for something lost. There was a spark with Jessica. He'd felt it that first day in the rain. But once again, things were not as they seemed. The man he killed in front of her house was guilty of bad judgment, nothing more. Actually, he was relieved. She was a complication. He felt a spark with her, but what he felt for Maria was more like a forest fire.

In the few minutes he'd been talking to Jessica, the doctor had left. Maria sat by the bed. Pete was asleep and his chest wrapped in bandages. He gently closed the door.

She stood and he gently gathered her into his arms and held her. She gripped him tightly and sobbed into his shoulder. They stayed that way for several minutes until she finally released him.

"He's going to be okay?"

She picked up a clean rag and wiped his shirt front.

"Sorry, I made a mess of your shirt. And yes, he's okay. He should pull through unless something happens." Shaking him fiercely by one arm, she stared into his eyes.

"He's too old for this, Coble. The only reason he's here is because of you. You're his friend, and even more importantly, you are like a son to him. This has to stop. Promise me. It has to stop!"

He slumped into the chair. Caleb was dead, and they'd nearly lost Pete. And whether she knew it or not, she was right. It had to end. He was tired, and tired of it. Deep bone tired.

She straddled his legs, facing him as she settled onto his lap. "It is not your fault. Pete loves this life too. You are both fools." She put her hands on his face, turning him to face her. "I'm a fool, too. I love you both."

He looked at her sharply, and she gave a little laugh. "Sorry, I can't help how I feel."

He sat holding her, and she kissed him. It was slow, thorough, and sensuous, leaving no doubt in his mind how she felt.

When he still didn't say anything, she shook her head. "You sure don't talk much, do you? But that's all right. You may not feel that way about me yet. I'll give you a little time. Just don't go running to that Jezebel woman. She has enough men. There has been enough killing, and I cannot give you children if I'm in jail."

He thought of the conversation in the hall. "I don't think you have to worry."

"What? Which part? You won't go to that woman, or I won't go to jail? And for the record...I really don't want to go to jail."

He abruptly stood, nearly dumping her on the floor. She looked startled and a little afraid, so he reached out and touched her cheek. "I'm not as immune to you as you think."

She giggled. "You think I don't know that? Honey, I've been sitting on your lap, remember?"

He smiled back and shrugged. "Don't count on the little ranch with kids running around the yard just yet. The next few days are going to be crazy. I've things to do. You may not like me so much after I'm done. Things are going to happen a little differently than normal. Your job is to take care of Pete. I'll send someone to help spell you. Keep your pistol handy. Don't let anyone in the door that you don't know. Especially that crazy-ass preacher."

She reached out for him as he turned to go. "Coble? You're scaring me. What...what are you going to do?"

"This has gone on long enough. I'm going to take care of business, just like always."

———

IT WAS full-dark when he walked into the saloon. Walking up to the bar, the first person he saw was Pop Janus.

Pop turned and held out his hand. "Sorry about Caleb. He was a good man."

He nodded as he shook Pop's hand. "Yes, he was. You've got him laid out at the undertakers?"

"Yeah. Miz Davis is taking care of it. We're going to bury him at the cemetery tomorrow afternoon. I reckon, since he's a lawman, there won't be a large crowd. Far as I know, there's no family."

"There isn't. Do me a favor. This isn't over yet. Can you and a few of your friends take care of guarding Pete's room? Maria's with him, and he's going to mend, but he needs rest. No one goes in without her permission. I don't want someone to come along and finish the job. Can you do that?"

"Got a few friends." Pop nodded his assent. "We'll be glad to."

He continued. "I need to talk to Isaiah Jakes. Can you make that happen?"

"Well, I can do that without any magic at all." He indicated a dimly lit corner of the room. "He's over there nursing a beer and his ill temper."

He snapped his gaze back to Pop. "Is he a drinker?"

Pop laughed. "If anyone had to depend on his drinking to make a living, they'd starve. He'll nurse the same beer all evening. Probably he doesn't want to go home and tell his woman no one's been brought to account for the death of his daughter."

"Hang on to your hat, Pops. That's about to change."

He picked up a beer and moved to the table. "Care if I join you?"

"Have a seat." The man looked at him curiously. "You got business with me?"

"Maybe." He looked closely and was glad to see the man wasn't drunk. "I need someone to do some babysitting."

Jakes sat up straighter. "You'll have to explain that, although I've got enough young'uns to have some experience at that."

He laid out the first part of his plan for him. "I'm a straightforward man. I've been treating this whole problem with the murders like some kind of puzzle, even when I have a good idea who's responsible. Don't ask me how. It's just a gut feeling. So I'm going to bust down some doors and arrest Sheriff Stiles for the murder of the Indian boy and Caleb. I'm also going to arrest the Reverend Stone for the murder of four girls, including your daughter."

Jakes folded his hands on the table, his beer forgotten. "Just how do I fit into this? I'm not a gunfighter, but I want that man dead."

"No, you're not a gunfighter, but you'll stand hitched if trouble comes. I'm going to throw them into jail, and I need a jailer. Once I get them into jail, no one goes in or out without my say-so."

There was a distinct twinkle in Isaiah's eyes. "How long? I might get hungry."

"I'll start tomorrow, and it should be over by the end of the day if I have things figured right. We'll put Caleb to rest tomorrow afternoon. Things will come to a head soon after."

"All right. When do you plan to gather up these sinners?"

He thought a moment. "First thing in the morning."

Isaiah reached over, retrieved his Sharps from the corner, and checked the load. "What are you doing right now? You need your beauty sleep?"

Well, now.

Chapter Seventeen

THE REVEREND STONE STAYED IN A SMALL HOUSE close behind the church when he was in town. He sat on the single bed, lost in thought. He'd tried going out at dark, but every trail had people on it. He could get past them easily enough, but couldn't be sure he could go anywhere with the next girl he'd chosen. There were just too many ways it could go wrong and he was a careful man.

He'd been holding a cup of water, but his hands shook so badly the water sloshed out, so he slung it across the room and into the wall.

Coble Bray.

Damn him!

The man had taken one look at him, and he knew. *Knew*! It was in his eyes. The loathing. The hatred. For a moment, he'd been afraid the marshal would shoot him on the spot.

And Jessica. She was a fine piece, and he thought he had a chance with her, but now she looked at him differently. Now she wondered about him. He could tell by her gaze, by her expression. And the sharp-eyed Captain Meyers watched him wherever he went. Anytime he got close to Jessica, the man was always there.

Damn. Damn. *Damn*!

He stood and threw clothes into a duffel bag. It was time to leave. There were other fields. Other flowers to be picked. Just as he turned toward the door, it slammed open, splintering as it tore off its hinges.

———

COBLE AND ISAIAH headed toward the church.

"There's a little shack behind the church the good reverend uses when he's in town," Isaiah said. "This time of night, he should be there. If he's not, we'll round him up somewhere."

As they stepped off the boardwalk into the street, a man came up close to them. "Looks like you're on a mission, Marshal."

"Captain Meyers," Coble responded. "We're about to round up some sinners, as Isaiah would say, and show them the error of their ways. Care to join us?"

Meyers chuckled in the darkness. "I just happen to be wearing my sidearm. This should be fun."

As they reached the shack, Coble indicated Isaiah should go around the back just in case there was more than one door. "Don't kill him unless you have to."

Standing in front of the house, it was easy to hear the reverend mumbling and cursing inside.

Meyers spoke in a whisper. "Do you want me to knock—"

Coble kicked in the door.

With a feminine-sounding screech, Finias Stone backed away from the door holding a duffel bag. "What's the meaning of this? You can't come in here."

Coble moved up close. "Yes, I can. I'm arresting you for the murder of the four girls."

Reverend Stone flinched, then relaxed and smiled. "You'll look the fool, Marshal. You've no proof."

"We'll see," Coble said.

The reverend turned to move away when Isaiah pushed the barrel of his Sharps about two inches into the man's stomach. "Stand still."

In a move nearly too quick to see, the reverend pulled a knife from behind his collar and swiped it at Isaiah, slashing his arm and making him drop the rifle.

Coble started to draw his pistol, but Captain Meyers beat him to it. He swiped the barrel of his Dragoon Colt across the reverend's head. The dragoon was a big, heavy pistol, and the reverend collapsed like a sack of potatoes.

They bound up Isaiah's arm and he walked outside. Then they tied up the reverend. As they dragged him outside, Isaiah showed up with a horse. "I'm not going to drag his ass all the way down to the jail."

"Smart man." Coble helped the captain toss the unconscious preacher on the horse's back.

"Who's next?" Meyers asked. "I'm getting a feel for this."

As they walked, leading the horse, Coble said, "We're going to the jail, and then I'm going to put the sheriff in one of his own cells."

"Interesting," was all Captain Meyers said.

———

THERE WAS a light showing in the jail since it was still early. They peeked inside. Stiles lay on his bunk reading a paper. Two other men sat at the desk playing cards. A half-empty bottle of whiskey stood between them.

After a short conference, Captain Meyers yelled, "In the jail. We have a man hurt out here."

Standing by the window, Coble watched the deputies pull their weapons and walk to the door. Sheriff Stiles didn't move. As the men came out, they encountered Meyers and Isaiah with the reverend slung over the horse.

"Who ya got there?" One of the men moved forward.

As they cleared the door, Coble slipped inside. He'd let the others take care of the deputies. "Evening, Sheriff."

Stiles shot up off the bunk, reaching for his gun.

"I wouldn't." He hadn't drawn his Colt, but was ready. "You said you were better than me. Would you care to try?"

Stiles relaxed. "Nah, you're too keyed up and ready. Your time will come."

There were grunts and groans from outside, and the two deputies were dragged in by their collars.

Stripped to their underwear to ensure there were no hidden weapons or keys, all the men were thrown into the cells, their clothes tossed in after them. Isaiah cleaned the desk off with a sweep of his hand, paper, and wanted posters littering the floor. He methodically took a couple of shotguns and a Henry repeater off the gun rack and loaded them.

"Turn off the lamp when you're through, and lock the doors behind us," Coble said. "Try and get some sleep. I'll be back in the morning. Do you need to see the doctor about that arm?"

Isaiah shook his head. "I've been cut worse shaving. So what are you going to do in the morning?"

He smiled grimly. "Why, tomorrow I'm going to find Texas Johnny Cade and Chico Cruz. When I find them, I'll read to them from the Book." With a last look at the men in the cell, he turned and left.

He paused on the veranda and overheard the men inside.

"Read to them from the book? I'm not familiar with that," Captain Meyers asked Isaiah.

"Why, I expect Marshal Bray will instruct the

sinners on the errors of their ways, like the Bible says to do. And then he's gonna kill them peckerwoods for what they did to his friend."

"I don't think the Bible says that."

Isaiah snorted. "Depends which book you read."

Coble stepped off the veranda and into the dusty street, thinking about what he'd just heard. Isaiah was wrong. Tomorrow, he might just shoot first and instruct later if need be.

———

COBLE WAS UP BEFORE DAWN, walking into the restaurant. There weren't many people there and he quietly ordered a cup of coffee. As he sat staring out the window, Maria came to his table. He stood and held her chair for her. She was pale and looked tired.

"How's Pete?"

She ran her fingers through her hair and smiled at him. "He is awake and asking for food. He'll be fine in a few days." She put her hand on his arm. "Thanks for sending Pops to watch the door. A couple of men came by last night, but he sent them on their way. I think that Greener shotgun had a lot to do with them leaving. Plus, one of his friends was sitting down the hall with a rifle."

"I figured someone might be by." He filled her in on all that had happened the evening before. "Now all I have to do is find Johnny Cade and Chico."

"Why? Why you? Can't you let the Army take care of it? I don't want to lose you."

"It's my job. You know that. Pete knows that."

"Then quit. When Pete heals, we can go somewhere and start over."

He looked at this beautiful woman, wondering how he could get so lucky. "After today, you may get your wish. We'll see how it goes."

"Make it today. Quit now. I have an excellent dowry. You don't need to work."

"It is not about money. You know that. I must finish this. Those men will be a danger to all of us if allowed to go free."

She looked at him closely. "You're planning something, aren't you? You seem...settled, for lack of a better word, and calm. Your plans are laid out in your mind and you're just waiting to execute them."

"Execute?" He smiled. "Sometimes you just have to let things play out."

Their conversation was interrupted with the entrance of the judge and his adjutant. They both nodded to him as they sat and ordered their meal.

He continued talking to Maria until the waitress brought a tray of food for Pete. When she stood to take it, he asked. "We're burying Caleb this afternoon. Will you be there?"

She shook her head. "I'm sure he was a good man, but I did not know him, and Pete can't go, so I'll stay with him. You understand, don't you?"

He looked at her for a long minute, memorizing her face. "I understand."

She paused, tears in her eyes. "I'll see you later? Promise me?"

His gaze never left her eyes. "If I can."

"No." She shook her head violently. "Not good enough. You come to see me. Alive. Make it happen. Whatever you have to do. No doubts."

He watched until she was out of sight and then turned his attention to the judge, walking to their table. When the judge looked up, he said, "I made some arrests last night you might be interested in."

"Really?" The judge's tone was dismissive. "I hadn't heard."

"I arrested your duly appointed sheriff for murder. Texas Johnny Cade and Chico Cruz were two of the men who killed Caleb. Sheriff Stiles is pulling their strings and they worked for him. I'll be seeing them later today."

"Will you be arresting them too?" Lieutenant Evans asked.

He looked at Evans for the first time, barely acknowledging his presence. "If they wish. They'll have their chance."

The judge was finally over his surprise. "On what evidence did you arrest the sheriff?"

"He admitted to me about killing the Indian boy. The rest of it is common knowledge."

The judge examined his coffee cup before raising his gaze to Coble. "Did anyone else hear this so-called confession? Anyone at all?"

"Nope."

"So it's your word against his." The judge shook his head. "He will go free and you know it."

"Maybe, but very soon, the community will know why he was arrested. Caleb was very well-liked. Then it won't matter if he goes to trial or not. I'm thinking he won't have a job long."

"I'll have a hearing on this matter today!" The judge's voice was furious. "You can't get away with this. Who else did you arrest?"

He smiled at them, relishing the moment. "The good Reverend Finias Stone for the murders of four girls."

The judge was stunned for a moment. "You're out of your mind. What's your evidence for that? And you'd better have some."

"He admitted it to me. And for me, that's good enough."

"That is preposterous. He would never do something like that. He's a man of God."

"Wouldn't do the crime or admit to the crime?" Coble chuckled. "I think he's more a disciple of a fallen angel than having any affinity to God. The man is the worst kind of monster."

A voice spoke from behind him. "You're insane."

He turned to find Jessica staring at him, her hands on her hips. Obviously on her way to breakfast, she'd overheard them.

"Finias wouldn't harm a fly," she said. "He's a man of honor and has the highest morals. You've completely lost your mind."

"Possibly." He smiled at her. "But I don't think so."

He left the judge and Lieutenant Evans staring at their cold food and Jessica speechless, which he figured was quite a feat considering her penchant for talking. The day was starting off well. Standing on the boardwalk a moment, he enjoyed the cool breeze coming down the valley from between the hills. The sun was up, but still hadn't touched the street and it lay in shadow.

Taking another deep breath, he headed to the jailhouse. There were already a few people crowded around the front door. As he approached, they parted to give him room.

Coble spoke sharply to them. "You people stay away from the front of the jail. Isaiah, let me in."

There was the sound of a bar being lifted, then the door opened. He ducked inside and the prisoners started yelling at him at once.

Isaiah grinned. "They didn't have a restful night, I'm afraid."

"Why don't you go and get something to eat. I'll watch the guests for a while."

Isaiah nodded. "I could eat. Listening to all this whining and complaining makes a man hungry."

After he left, Captain Meyers came through the door. "Any trouble?"

"Not so far. Do me a favor and hold that hand-cannon of yours on the sheriff. I'm going to let his two deputies go."

He unlocked the door, watching Stiles closely.

After the two men were out, he told them, "I don't want to see either of you again. Get your gear, your horses, and leave the country. And I mean leave it. If I see you again, I'll just naturally figure you're looking for me and I'll kill you. Understood?"

They mumbled a couple of "yes sirs" and left. In their haste, one stumbled and fell over the edge of the boardwalk. Coble grimly watched them head toward the livery.

Captain Meyers stood beside him. "I thought you were going to look for Cade and Cruz this morning?"

"Hell, Captain. I'm too lazy for that. Besides, I don't have a clue where they are. No, I'll let them come to me." He pointed at the two men leaving. "That's why I turned them loose. Those two know where the men are hiding and will do my job for me. I'll just wait."

"You're setting yourself up as a target in a shooting gallery. They'll back-shoot you."

He smiled. "Chico might. Cade won't. He wants my reputation. He'll brace me."

The captain shook his head. "Still, sounds like suicide to me."

"That's what they pay me for." He turned to the captain. "By the way, I thought you were supposed to be watching Perez?"

Meyers's eyes turned cold. "I'm lazy like you. After last night's little adventure, I got inspired. Perez and I had a little talk. He decided it was in his best interest to leave town before daylight. I believe he's on his way to visit an uncle in old Mexico."

Coble looked closely at the captain. There was a small abrasion on his cheek and his knuckles were skinned. "I'm surprised you got him to fight with his hands. I thought Perez was a gunman."

"Oh, he is. But the first thing they teach you at West Point is never let an opponent choose the terrain or the weapons. He wasn't much of a fighter, though. Folded like a wet tent."

———

AFTER ENLISTING Captain Meyers to go to the restaurant and order food trays for his prisoners, he went back inside.

Looking at the two remaining prisoners, he said, "I have food coming for you in a little bit."

The men were silent, but after a while, the reverend couldn't resist speaking. "When the judge lets me out, I'll come looking for you."

Coble laughed, shaking his head. "No, you won't. You'll slink into the forest like the skunk you are. I'm not a little girl. And if the judge does turn you loose, you won't have to come looking for me. I won't be far behind you. One question, though. Why? Why kill these young girls? It makes no sense to take the life of innocents."

Stone looked at him for a long moment, a small smile on his face. "I'm afraid it would take an amount of intelligence you don't possess to understand something like this. You simply don't have it. But think of this. Maybe I'm trying to save their innocence."

Coble continued to look at the man and wished Maria were here to decipher that last statement. Stone looked normal, except for the dead eyes. Somewhere inside, he was broken. Shaking his head, he gave up trying to talk. Words would come, but understanding would not.

"What about me?" the sheriff asked. "How long are you going to keep me locked up?"

He shrugged and shook his head. "Up to the judge. Far as I'm concerned, you'll hang. You had a good man killed. And for what? A little bank money? What?"

"You mean Caleb?" the sheriff replied. "He was too nosey and kept buttin' in the wrong places, but I'm not admitting to anything."

"You'll hang for killing the Indian boy."

"It's your word against mine. You know the judge won't hold me."

Coble nodded. "Maybe, but when the court takes the word of a petty thief like you over mine, it'll be time for me to retire."

"You'd better let me go. I got people coming soon. Once they get here, you'll be a dead man."

"I'm counting on that."

When he saw Isaiah and Captain Meyers returning with the food trays, he smiled at the prisoners. "Enjoy your last meal, gentlemen."

Chapter Eighteen

COBLE STOOD BY WHILE THE PRISONERS WERE given their food. Afterward, Isaiah came to stand by him on the boardwalk.

"Seems there are a couple of men over at the saloon getting some early courage from a bottle. They have some friends with them. Do you want some help with this?"

He glanced up the street. "No, I'd like you and Captain Meyers to stay out of it. However, if you were kind of standing by with your Sharps to make sure no one else interferes, I'd appreciate it."

"That I can do. Godspeed, Marshal Bray."

He went back inside and picked up the Greener shotgun. He checked the loads and looked a question at Isaiah.

"Double charge of powder, with buckshot and pennies." He grinned. "I loaded them myself."

MARIA STOOD by the window of Pete's room when she saw Coble leave the jail and move toward the saloon carrying a shotgun. She knew where he was headed. One of the housekeepers had told her Texas Johnny Cade, Chico Cruz, and a few of their friends were downstairs getting an early start with rotgut whiskey.

She turned and started toward the door, stopping to pick up her Colt and the one usually carried by Pete.

"No," Pete said hoarsely, reaching out his hand.

She turned to him instantly, surprised to hear him speak. "You're awake? I thought you'd sleep a while."

"I heard what the housekeeper told you. Girl, you can't help him now. He must do this on his own."

Looking at her father, sad at how frail he seemed, she said, "I have to. He's my man."

"All the more reason to not go down there. Right now, his only worry is himself. He will have told everyone to stay away. It's just his way. When the shooting starts, everyone he sees is an enemy. It keeps it simple. If you try to help, you'll be a distraction and might get him killed. You can't go."

She stared at her father a moment, then went to him. Sitting on the side of the bed, she hugged him gently. "I will be careful, but I'm going down there to make sure you have grandchildren. He's the one I want to father them, and I'll be damned if I'll let him be killed."

———

COBLE MET Pop coming out of the hotel and saloon.

"There are four of them inside," Pop said.

He stopped and looked around at the oldster. "How fond are you of that chair you've been riding?"

"What?"

"Give me about thirty seconds after I go inside, then I want you to toss it through the window."

The saloon was nearly deserted when he walked in. Not surprising. Most townspeople were smart enough to know something was going to happen. Cade and Chico stood at the bar, Cade laughing at some joke and Chico looked surly and morose. Two men he didn't know sat at a table, their rifles across the top of it.

All eyes turned to him as he moved through the door.

"You boys come in peaceful," Coble's voice rapped out. "I'm arresting you for the murder of Caleb McGill. There doesn't have to be any killing here."

The men at the table started to their feet, cursing as they bumped the table on their way up and the rifles skidded to the floor. As they reached for their pistols, the front window caved in with a loud crash.

The men whirled toward the new threat, and Coble fired at them with the shotgun. The roar of the double-barreled Greener was deafening in the confines of the large room. Both men were close together, so he aimed between them. The two went down screaming in pain as the buckshot and pennies tore into them.

His attention went back to the two at the bar. Chico's guns were coming up and Coble palmed his new Colt and fired. There was a searing pain in his shoulder. He'd been hit. For some reason, Cade hadn't drawn his weapon, so he concentrated on the other man. Powder smoke was thick in the room and his eyes stung. Chico's shirt was bloody.

Coble staggered back as a bullet sliced through the outside of his thigh and another hit the side of his gun belt and turned him. He thumbed the hammer on his last shot and put it in the middle of Chico's chest. The man stood there with a fixed smile on his face as his eyes glazed over. He went to one knee and tried to lift his gun. It fell from his fingers as he slowly fell forward, dead before he hit the floor.

Texas Johnny Cade was smiling and holding a gun on him. "Seems you are out of bullets."

"I'm not."

The voice came from Coble's left. Maria!

She spoke again. "I can't let you do this, Johnny. He's my man."

Cade looked at her, shook his head, and then slowly lowered his weapon. "Ah, hell. I couldn't shoot him now, anyway. He can't defend himself." He tipped his hat at Maria. "And I sure as hell can't shoot a beautiful woman like you." He backed toward the side door. "But I'll be back when you're mended, Coble. We have unfinished business. I'm faster than you, and I want everyone to know it."

Coble turned and suddenly had an arm full of Maria. He was bleeding all over her, but she kept her pistol trained on the side door Cade had just moved through.

"Load my pistols. Hurry, Maria. Right now."

She didn't argue, pulling brass shells from his belt, punching out the empties, and loading the cylinders, all the while casting a nervous glance at the side door.

A moment later, it opened, and Johnny Cade came back in, standing tall as the light from the open door framed him.

Coble pushed Maria to the side and faced him.

"I couldn't leave it." Cade shrugged. "I made my brag."

"Just let it go. You can walk away from this. There's no shame in it."

"Cain't." Texas Johnny Cade went for his gun.

The one shot was almost anticlimactic compared to what had gone on before. Cade stood, gun half-drawn, then crumpled to the floor. There was a small hole in his forehead.

"He was a good-looking boy," Maria said. "We'll put that on his tombstone."

———

ABRUPTLY, the room filled with people. Someone shoved a chair under Coble's legs and he sat. Maria held a compress on his shoulder and the bleeding slowed to a trickle.

She grabbed a waitress and told her. "Go tell Pete we're alright. He'll be wondering."

The bodies were dragged out and fresh sawdust thrown on the floor. Pop came in and inspected his chair, then came over to Coble.

"That was the fastest draw I ever saw."

Coble shook his head. "Had to. Maria was standing by me. I couldn't let him get off a shot."

She spoke in a soft voice. "I'm not sorry. Pete told me not to come, but I had to."

A few minutes later, the doctor had left and Coble sat at a table. Maria had gone up to be with Pete again. He was surprised to see the saloon fill up with people. But no one was drinking.

When most of the chairs were filled with people standing around the perimeter of the room, Judge Johnstone walked in with Lieutenant Evans.

They seemed to always be joined at the hip. Coble wondered idly if the young lieutenant was in the room that night with Jessica.

"Gentlemen," the judge said, "thanks for coming to this hearing on such short notice. It is a matter of great importance. The marshal has put two men in jail who are innocent of any wrongdoing. I will not entertain any testimony because I have already talked to Marshal Bray about this. He says Reverend Stone has admitted to killing the four girls, and strangely, that Sheriff Stiles has confessed to killing an unnamed Indian boy. That's a lot of confessing. I talked to both men this morning and they denied any involvement with either situation. Therefore, I will not hold them over for trial until proper evidence is provided."

The judge paused to swig some beer. "Since it's simple hearsay, the marshal's word against theirs, it's my duty to order the release of these men immediately. We will adjourn this meeting to the front of the jail."

Captain Meyers was at Coble's side to help him walk the short distance to the jail. "Coble, you're leaking all over the floor again. Do you know what this is all about?"

"Not a clue." He smiled. "Well, maybe a little."

At the jail, Coble called out, "Isaiah, open the door."

Isaiah poked his head out.

"Isaiah, I know this is hard, but you're going to have to trust me on this. Let the men out, unharmed."

"No." He shook his head. "No. He killed my little girl." Isaiah looked at the judge with haunted eyes. "He bragged about it."

"That is just hearsay and not admissible in court," the judge replied.

"I know it's hard," Coble said. "But the judge is letting them go. We can't stop it. Believe me, people who count will know what the judge has done.

Right now, you need to trust me and do what he says. Isaiah, I'm asking you to trust me."

Isaiah looked hard at him for a moment, then nodded and disappeared back inside.

When the two men came out, Coble and Captain Meyers found themselves surrounded by a squad from the cavalry detachment. They were quickly disarmed.

Judge Johnstone stepped forward, holding his hand out. "Mr. Bray, I'll have your badge, please."

Coble unhooked the star from his shirt with a small smile. The parting was a lot easier than he thought it would be. "Thank you, Judge."

Captain Meyers struggled in the grasp of his own men. Before him was Lieutenant Cahill. "I'll have your bars for this, you little weasel."

The lieutenant smirked at them both.

Coble put a restraining hand on Meyers's arm. "It's all right, Captain. I expected this. It's all part of the plan."

The man stopped struggling. "You have a plan? So far, I'm not seeing a real good plan here."

"Well, the best-laid plans of mice and men," Coble started.

Meyers finished. "Oft go awry."

The judge spoke again. "Have your soldiers release the captain and Mr. Bray, Lieutenant Evans. All we needed were their weapons and his badge. We just need to ensure they do not interfere." He turned to the other men. "Sheriff Stiles, since feelings are running high here in town, I'm ordering you to escort the reverend to the nearest railhead. As soon as you have him delivered safely, return here and resume your duties as sheriff. Do you understand?"

Sheriff Stiles smiled. "I understand. Thank you, Judge."

"Yes, thank you," Reverend Stone said. "If you will allow the sheriff to escort me to the hotel, there are some items I need to pick up. You might have them bring our horses to the back of the hotel. That way, we can avoid any more"—he grinned a Cheshire Cat grin—"hostilities."

"Maybe they should just leave right now, Judge. Directly from here," Coble said.

The judge looked at him oddly, and then, at his nod, the two parted the crowd and headed to the hotel.

Reverend Stone stopped and came back to stand in front of Coble.

They stared at each other a moment until the reverend spoke quietly. "You must know I'll just pick up where I left off. I've done it before. I will do it again. No one can stop me. There are many fields and many flowers. You came out a poor second on this one, and you always will. You cannot win. I'll continue."

"No. You won't," Coble said.

The reverend gave his little smile and went to join the sheriff.

———

CAPTAIN MEYERS PACED the ground angrily. "You're just going to let them go?"

"Unfortunately, the judge is right on this. I don't have any proof that'll stand up in court. Looking at it, there probably never will be. However, that doesn't mean they will not be punished."

The captain was about to reply when they heard a strangled cry. "Coble!"

He whirled and saw Pete leaning on a post in front of the hotel. His wounds had broken open and blood covered his chest.

"Maria," he choked out. "They took her."

Coble tried to keep the man from falling to the ground. "Who? Who took her? Baldknobbers?"

"It was that sheriff and the preacher," Pete said. "They just walked in and knocked her down. Then they tied her up and took her out. I-I tried to stop them."

Coble put a hand on Pete's arm. "It's okay. You're in no shape to do much good."

"And you are?" Pete tried to catch his breath. "You look like you've been shot to rag dolls."

Meyers said, "They must have gone straight west from the back of the hotel. We would have seen them if they'd used the main trail. Hang on a minute, I'll get some troopers and we'll go after them."

"No need." Coble watched the Indian riding in from the end of the street, whipping his horse and kicking it in the flanks with his heels.

The man skidded to a stop in front of them. "Wild Pony send me. He say come quick."

They grabbed their weapons that lay on the porch and then a couple of horses off the nearest hitching rail. They'd deal with the horse stealing charges later. Mounted, they took off after the Indian.

Entering the forest directly behind the hotel, they slowed to a fast walk, following a dimly defined trail up a hill and between two mountains. Sound was muted in the dense foliage, the only noise was the cadence of the hoof beats and creaking of saddle leather. No one spoke. They crossed a shallow creek bed of moss-covered rocks, canopied by towering sycamore and white oak. They silently followed the guide between a few more hills. About thirty minutes later, they came out into a small glade.

Maria stood to one side, beside a horse. Coble dismounted and went directly to her. Her blouse had buttons missing and she tried to hold it together with one hand while she held onto him with the other.

At his expression at seeing her blouse torn, she quickly told him, "I'm all right. This was torn trying to get away from them. There wasn't time for anything else."

He looked at Wild Pony for confirmation and got it. With a sigh of relief, he hugged her to him.

He didn't look at the sheriff or the reverend. At least ten warriors surrounded them. He looked at Wild Pony, then reached up and shook his hand.

"Thank you, my friend. I owe you. Anytime. Anyplace."

The Indian whirled his horse and joined the group. The two captives were quickly trussed up and separated.

Ignoring the sheriff, Coble walked over to the reverend. On the way, he nodded at Wild Pony and got a nod in return. It was enough. A message conveyed and answered. He stood looking at the reverend a moment before he spoke.

"Jenny Slocum. Faith James. Elaine Davis. Isabel Jakes. God knows how many others." He shook his head. "You killed Elaine Davis and then bedded her mother. What kind of sick—well, it's beyond my comprehension."

"Captain!" The reverend looked past Coble. "I'm glad you are here. You can take me into custody. Take me to trial. I admit everything. You'll be famous for bringing me in. Please."

"Captain Meyers." Coble turned briskly away from the prisoners. "I want to thank you for helping me find Maria." He glanced at her and she did that one eyebrow thing. "We had a lovers' quarrel and she ran away. She's a little skittish around men, but hopefully I'll have her whipped into shape soon. Isn't that right, Maria?"

She gave him a long look, but didn't reply.

He turned his back on the warriors and helped Maria to her horse.

Taking one quick look behind him, the captain nodded. "Always my pleasure to help, Coble. These little disagreements are common, or at least..." He grinned. "I've heard they are with young, immature women."

Maria was growling by this time.

As they were all mounted and guided their horses back the way they'd come, she finally spoke. "You're just going to leave them out here?"

"Who?" both men answered in unison.

Chapter Nineteen

LATER THAT EVENING, WHEN THE SHADOWS WERE long and the whippoorwills called down the valley, a few friends of Caleb McGill gathered at his grave-side. No hymns were sung or speeches given. He was laid to rest with no fanfare. It was the way he would have wanted it.

Coble looked at the few people standing with him. "I don't know all the religious beliefs represented here. I can only tell you what Caleb and I believe. He would ask you not to stand and mourn his passing. He is not here and does not sleep. His spirit is alive and well. His troubles are over, and who knows what adventures are ahead for him?

"In Caleb's stead, I want to thank each of you for coming. We, each of us, would have liked to say goodbye to him. But that's not the way the world works. We don't control when we come into this world, and rarely have any say when we leave it. He was a good man. That's epitaph enough."

———

LATER, Jessica stood next to her daughter's grave when Coble joined her. She looked at him a moment before she finally spoke. "That was a wonderful farewell for Caleb. He would have enjoyed it. I'm sorry I talked Caleb into sending for you. I can't help feeling he would be alive if I hadn't been so selfish."

He shrugged. "It's hard to tell. Lawmen make enemies. But you could be right."

She sighed. "So much killing, and none of it brought her back or eased the pain of her passing. So much killing, and nothing has changed."

"Something *did* change. A killer was caught. He'll pay, and very soon I'm thinking."

"Who will? For which crime? I still don't believe Finias Stone killed my daughter, and I'm not convinced Sheriff Stiles had anything to do with Caleb's death. Even if you are correct, the reverend's gone and the sheriff won't be back anytime soon."

Coble nodded. "Well, you're entitled to your opinion. Before you write that opinion in stone, talk to Captain Meyers about it. You might change your mind. As far as the decision goes, I'll just have to live with it."

"And you lost your star over it. A job you believed in. I'm sorry for that."

As they talked, they moved away from Caleb's grave. "Don't be. It was high time for me to go."

Jessica chuckled. "Your little Mexican?"

He just grinned at her. "She wants a lot of kids."

Giving a very unladylike snort, she extended her arm to Captain Meyers. "Captain, would you escort me home? There are a lot of unfriendly people about, and Mr. Bray thinks you have information I might want."

Patting her on the arm and leading her away, Captain Meyers turned with a smile and shrugged at Coble.

———

A SHORT WALK found him back at the hotel, entering his room. He took his left arm out of the sling and moved his shoulder around. It hurt, but was still serviceable. The bullet from Johnny Cade had entered the muscle just above the collarbone. Right next to an older scar. He threw the sling on the bed and put on a clean shirt. Miraculously, all his clothes were washed and pressed. It didn't take him long to pack.

Holding his duffel and rifle in one hand, he stopped at Pete's room. A middle-aged woman giggled and exited as soon as he came in.

"Well, it looks like you're in good hands." He chuckled. "Quite literally."

Pete turned a bright shade of red, which was quite a feat with his sun-bronzed skin.

"She's my nurse."

"And a damned good one she is." Coble finally just laughed and sat in the only chair. "Time for me to go, old friend. I met the judge on the street and he's looking daggers at me. It seems the town folk want me gone. It's funny. Once you do the job they ask of you, they always want you gone."

Pete sat up. "It's always been the same. You know that. People are afraid to stand up for themselves. Then when you do it for them, you remind them of their failings. Too much killing. People can't separate the good you do from the evil the outlaws do."

He shook Pete's hand. "Adios, partner. Come to KC when you are up to it and I'll buy you a beer."

"Nah. I'm going back to the ranch, and I may take that nurse with me. I'm pretty beat up and need a lot of attention. I kinda thought you'd be heading our way, listening to Maria talk."

"Have you seen her?"

"She left. That was a good piece of work downstairs. I'm curious. How'd you know Johnny Cade would come back?"

"It was his nature. He had to. There just was not any other way it could play out. And Maria?"

"She brought this nurse in, told me she was leaving, and then said she'd see me as soon as she could."

Coble thought a moment, an empty feeling in his stomach, and then shrugged. "She didn't much like how things turned out. Well, maybe she'll turn up. *Hasta*, Pete. I'll see you."

"You take care of my girl."

"Given the chance, I will." Coble grinned. "But damned if I call you Daddy!"

————

COBLE STOPPED off in the saloon when he saw Pops at the bar. He leaned next to him. "Thanks for the help. Your timing was excellent."

"Glad to help. I'd about worn that chair out anyway. You heading out?"

"Yeah. I may be back, though." He looked around and out the windows. "I have some unfinished business here."

Pop laughed. "I haven't seen Maria lately, if that's your unfinished business. That's a fine girl. Don't mess that up."

"Mess it up? Pops, I haven't had a say in that since I met her."

"With women, you never do. Say, there was a young man in here a while ago. I think his name was Sandy. He said he'd get your horse for you so you wouldn't have to walk far, since you're wounded and all. Nice young feller."

Just as he was leaving, a young man came in the door dressed in jeans, a checkered shirt, and a cowhide vest, with a floppy hat pulled down low.

He was gonna have to break her of that.

No guns were visible, but he knew there had to be at least one hidden somewhere. Maybe someday soon he'd find out where.

Walking right up to him, Sandy grabbed the

front of his shirt, pulled his head down, and planted a lingering kiss on his lips, then stepped back.

"That damned horse still bites," she told him. The silence in the barroom was deafening.

He chuckled and followed Sandy out the door. He still liked that walk. As he was about to walk out the door, he heard the speculation break out behind him.

"Did that ranny just come in and kiss the deacon on the lips?"

"I seen that."

"You think he's...?"

"Don't know. Ain't gonna ask him, either."

Chapter Twenty

IT WAS A WEEK AFTER THEY LEFT BIG SPRINGS when Coble and Maria entered the little church in Kansas City. He wore a broadcloth suit and she had on a print dress with lace around the collar and wrists. They were both uncomfortable in the new clothes, but at least he had found where she hid her gun.

The church looked the same as when he had left it earlier. Not that much time had passed. He walked down the aisle the same as before, feeling the smooth wood of the pews, smelling dust and linseed oil. The sun coming through the windows gave the same dusty light for those within.

She followed him but paid more attention to the stained-glass windows and the altar at the front. "This is a beautiful church. They probably have a lot of weddings here."

"We'll meet Priest in a moment." He'd already seen Pastor Schuler coming in the side door and spoke loudly. "He's mean and ugly, but a kind old man for all of that."

"So, he's Catholic?" Maria asked.

"No, ma'am," Pastor Schuler answered, startling her. "I'm German Lutheran. Pastor August Schuler." He shook her hand and looked over at Coble. "I used to be a friend of Coble's when he was still a marshal." The two men shook hands.

"So this is Maria. The one who made you retire. She's beautiful. A wedding is in the near future?"

"Well."

"Yes." Maria gave Coble an evil eye. "Very soon. All we need is a church and a priest." She smiled at him then. "Or a pastor."

After a few minutes of small talk, catching up on the happenings around town and all that had happened at Big Springs, Pastor Schuler said, "I have a letter for you that came today. It was a dispatch rider from the Army."

Coble looked at the envelope a moment, then handed it to Maria. "Would you read it to us, please?"

They sat on the pews as she tore it open. "Oh. It is from Captain Meyers."

I hope this post finds you and Maria well. I am still seeing Jessica, but that seems to be cooling somewhat. I am not sure what she is looking for, but since the death of her husband and daughter, she seems to have some proclivities I do not understand.

At raised eyebrows from Priest, Coble said, "Later."

Some interesting developments have come up since you left. You might be interested to know that Sheriff Stiles never came back to his duties at Big Springs. When he was overdue, Judge Johnstone, who seemed very perplexed, sent us out to look for him. He was not hard to find. All we had to do was follow the buzzards. Being from Apache country, I am sure you can visualize the scene. We found the sheriff spread-eagled on an ant hill. He was scalped and his belly cut open. The carrion birds and ants had been at him before we found him, but our scout believes he lived for quite some time. By the way, our scout is the fellow who helped Wild Pony bring in Caleb and Pete. Seems he saw that Otoe girl Wild Pony's son was after, and now he needs a job to buy ponies. Strange, but Wild Pony would not give up his. I'd like to hear the conversation around that campfire.

We also found Finias Stone in a similar manner. Our scout seemed to know just where to look. The good reverend was tied to the top of a rock. He was wrapped in buckskin from head to toe, even over his eyes, so the birds and animals could not get to him. The exception was the area covering his genitals. An opening was cut there, and he was bloodied to draw in the animals. We believe he lived for quite some time. With his eyes covered, he would have been in darkness the whole time. It was a hideous way to go.

They do say there was a cross woven from

grapevines put by the rock, so it cannot have been Indians. They would never do that.

There was some mention of Wild Pony being in the area. I assured everyone concerned that I know the man and he was still in Indian Territory, Oklahoma.

The judge is still in the area, but I have heard rumors that he will be recalled to Ft. Smith soon. Somehow, word of his actions in Big Springs has reached his superiors. No one has seen his adjutant, Mr. Evans. I just happen to have his signed resignation on my desk, but he seems to have left the country.

Life goes on.

I remain your obedient servant,
David Meyers, Captain, USA

"You were sure?" Priest asked. "Hideous does not describe how those two men died."

Coble nodded after a moment. "Both confessed."

Priest turned his cold gray eyes on Coble. "Do you still want to argue predestination?"

"No," Coble replied, remembering their last conversation. Then he smiled. "But the clarity of it points me to a small ranch in Oklahoma."

"After the wedding," Maria said.

Coble sighed. "After the wedding."

It was the first time he'd ever seen Priest smile.

A Look at Book Two:

Hard Times

In the shadow of a deal with the devil, a retired lawman faces a killer's deadly game.

Legendary lawman Coble Bray's world changes when he meets the fiery Maria. Leaving his gunslinger life behind, they settle into a peaceful existence on a small Missouri ranch. But tranquility is a luxury Coble can't afford for long.

When an old comrade, Priest, arrives with news of a brutal murder, Coble's past beckons him back to the badge. The victim was found with a chilling message—a cross and key in her mouth, along with a note addressed to Coble, hinting at the work of a sinister figure connected to an unsolved murder the previous year.

Driven by duty and haunted by the threat of a serial killer, Coble steps into the fray, where his quest leads him to Hard Times, Kansas—a town as foreboding as his circumstances. There, he finds himself alone, playing a perilous game with a murderer who's always one step ahead.

Can Coble Bray outwit a devilish adversary, or will his final showdown cost him everything he holds dear?

AVAILABLE JUNE 2024

About the Author

Darrel Sparkman is an award-winning author of novels, novellas, and short stories. He's been included in three western anthologies, worked as a feature writer for *Saddlebag Dispatches* and blogged a short time for *Sundown Press*.

His ideas come from a diverse past of serving as a combat search and rescue helicopter crewman in Vietnam and volunteer Emergency Medical Technician First Responder. He has worked as a professional photographer, computer repair tech, and was once part-owner of a commercial greenhouse operation and flower shop.

Darrel is enjoying semi-retirement and finally has that job that wakes him up every day—with a smile on his face.